The · Bog · of · Stars

THE·BOG·OF STARS

And Other Stories
. and Sketches .
of Elizabethan Ireland

By STANDISH O'GRADY

Short Story Index Reprint Series

BOOKS FOR LIBRARIES PRESS
FREEPORT, NEW YORK

First Published 1893
Reprinted 1970

STANDARD BOOK NUMBER:
8369-3601-9

LIBRARY OF CONGRESS CATALOG CARD NUMBER:
74-125234

PRINTED IN THE UNITED STATES OF AMERICA

PREFACE

THE following stories are not so much founded on fact as in fact true. The events are in each case related either as they actually occurred or with a very slight dramatization and infusion of local and contemporaneous colour. My object generally has been to bring the modern Irish reader into closer and more sympathetic relation with a most remarkable century of Irish history ; a century which, more than any other, seems to have determined the destiny of Ireland.

S. O'G.

CONTENTS

THE BOG OF STARS

MONA-REULTA

" Bog " is not a beautiful word though melodious
Milton found a place for it in his *Paradise Lost*.
It sounds better in Gaelic, for it is pronounced
bogue, and means " soft." The thing signified
has a doubtful reputation. Bogs are glorious in the
eyes of sportsmen, a valuable property when they
produce turf, and when they do not, blots on the
face of Nature, upon which the improver wages
constant war by drains, plantations, and other im-
provers' methods. On the whole bogs are not
popular, and yet sometimes at night, when stars
fill the sky, bogs reflect their glory. Then the
fowler, home-returning, tired and meditative, with
his tired dogs at his heels, pauses for a moment
beside some pool, and looks down and not up. It
is a feature of bogs which has not escaped the
notice of our poet, Mr. W. B. Yeats—

> " Where the wandering water gushes
>   In the hills above Glencar,
>   In pools amongst the rushes
>   That scarce could bathe a star."

The old name-makers of Ireland noticed it too.
There is an Irish bog called Mona-Reulta, or the

Bog of Stars. Don't ask me to place it upon the map; probably it has long since yielded to the assiduous improver, and now grows corn for man and green grass for cattle, and is not starry any more. All I know is that it flourished once and was starry, and figures in a tale known lang syne, but improved out of memory, as probably Mona-Reulta itself has been.

The golden time of great Eliza was drawing towards its close, when in the dusk of a January evening an army issued from the massive gateway of a castle court-yard, and took the road, headed by a file of fifers and a drum. The fifers played a brisk old Irish air, and the drummer drummed as if he had a great deal of do-nothing weariness to work out of his arms and wrists. Then in well-scoured pots and shining jacks came many files of gunmen. Smoke exhaled from this part of the army—not tobacco smoke, though an odd pipe may have been lighting there too—but the smoke of burning tow-match, which for each soldier was coiled round the stock of his piece. Pikemen followed, also in head-pieces and breast-pieces, with their long, slender weapons on their shoulders, aslope, making a beautiful sight. Rough garrans with rougher drivers succeeded them, the garrans laden with panniers. On the backs of some of the garrans were fastened ladders, newly made, for they were very white. Then came a promiscuous crowd of

bare-headed, long-haired youths, in tight trews and
saffron-coloured tunics, who skipped to the music,
singing their own songs too as an accompaniment.
Each had a sword on his thigh, and a bundle of
light spears in his hands ; mantles of many bright
hues surrounded their shoulders, rolled after the
manner of a Highlander's plaid. They were the
Queen's kerne ; a young English gentleman commanded them, not without difficulty. More gunmen
and pikemen followed, bringing up the rear. It
was a small army—only a few hundred men—yet
a fairly large one for the times, and a well-equipped
one too, fit to do good service to-night if all go
well. Some ten or a dozen horsemen accompanied
this army, all in complete armour, some in gilded
armour. They went in twos and threes together,
or rode from front to rear, keeping a sharp eye on
the moving host. This army marched keeping its
back to the sea and its face to the mountains. Two
men rode together near the band, which was now
silent ; the fifers were shaking the wet out of their
fifes.

"What dost thou surmise, Tom ?" said one in
gilded armour to the other, whose armour was only
iron and not bright. "Shall we catch the wily
Raven in his nest this night ?" The speaker was
Lord Deputy of Ireland.

"My lord, I am sure of it," answered the duller
soldier. "My scouts report all quiet in the glen.

The Raven has not fifty men with him, and suspects nothing. Pick up thy drumsticks there. 'Swounds, man, what sort of drummer art thou to drum for the Queen's soldiers? Your Honour, the Raven is thine this night, alive or dead.'' Now the band struck up again, the drummer drummed, and the remainder of this conversation was lost to all but the speakers. By the way, why did that drummer drop his drumsticks? Had the knight addressed as Tom (his full style was Captain Thomas Lee) known *that,* there would have been a different issue of this well-planned '' draught,'' and my story would never have been written, or the Bog of Stars celebrated.

The drummer youth drummed almost as well as before that overheard conversation about the Raven had shaken the drumsticks from his hand. The sub-conscious musical soul in him enabled him to do that; but his thoughts were not in the music. Something then said caused to pass before him an irregular dioramic succession of mental scenes and pictures. For him, as he whirred with his little drumsticks, or sharply rat-at-at-ated, memory and imagination, on blank nothing for canvas, and with the rapidity of lightning, flung pictures by the hundred. Here is one for a sample : it passed before him like a flash, but passed many times. A long table, a very long table, spread for supper, redolent of supper, steaming with supper, and he very willing to sup. Vessels of silver, of gold too—

for it was some gala night—shone in the light of many candles. Rows of happy faces were there, and one face eminent above all. There were candles in candlesticks of branching silver, or plain brass, or even fixed in jars and bottles. All the splendour was a good way off from him. He was at the wrong end of the long table, but he was there. At his end was no snow-white linen, and the cups and platters were only of ash or wild apple ; but of good food there was plenty, and of ale too, for such as were not children. It was the supper table of a great lord. The boy was at one end, and the great lord at the other, he was at one end and the Raven at the other. He was not kin to this great lord, whom he called Clan-Ranal, and to whom he was too young to do service. He knew no mother, and hardly remembered his father ; he had been slain, they told him, "when Clan-Ranal brake the battle on the Lord Deputy and all the Queen's Host."

Again, in imagination, the drummer-boy sat in Clan-Ranal's glowing hall while the storm raged without, and shook the clay-and-timber sides of that rude palace. There sat the swarthy chief, beaming good-will and hospitality upon all. His smiles, and the flash of his kind eyes illuminated the hall from end to end, and made the food sweeter and the ale stronger. He was only a robber chief, but oh, so great ! so glorious ! in the child's eyes. His " queen " was at his right hand, and around him

his mighty men of valour, famous names, sung by
many bards, names that struck terror afar through
the lowlands. To the boy they were not quite
earthly ; he thought of them with the supernatural
heroes of old time. He did not know that his
" king " was a robber, or, if he did, thought that
robbery was but another name for celerity, boldness,
and every form of warlike excellence, as in such
primitive Homeric days it mostly is. To others,
the Raven and his mighty men were sons of death
and perdition ; but their rapine sustained him, and
in their dubious glory he rejoiced. A fair child's
face, too, mingled always in these scenes and
pictures, which chased each other across the mind
of the drummer. He saw her, in short green kirtle
and coat of cloth-of-gold, step down from the king's
side at an assembly, bearing to him, the small but
distinguished hurler of toy spears, the prize of excellence (it was only a clasp knife ; he had it still),
and saw her sweet smile as she said, " Thou will
do some great deed one day, O Raymond, Fitz
Raymond, Fitz Pierce." All the gay, bright happy
life of his childhood, so happy because it held so
much love, came and went in flashes before his
gazing eyes ; and now he drummed on the army
which was to quench in blood, in horrors unspeak-
able and unthinkable, the light of that happy home
where he had once been so happy himself. Tears
ran down the drummer's face, unseen, for the

night had now come. Then a thought, a purpose, flashed swiftly, like a meteor, across his mind, and came again less transiently, and then came to stay, fixed, clear, and determinate ; a purpose like a star. He drummed better after that, and spoke as stoutly as his fellows about the glorious achievement which was to be performed that night, and about his share of the plunder. Yet his thoughts were not plunderous, but heroic. He, Raymond, son of Raymond, son of Pierce, son of, etc., etc., would do a great deed that night. Some pride of birth may have mingled with the lad's purpose, for he was of a sept broken and scattered indeed, but once famous—the Fitz-Eustaces. He knew his genealogical line by heart. If there was a drummer at one end of it, there was an earl at the other.

The two horsemen conversed once more. "Where are we now, Tom?" exclaimed the leader of the draught.

"Your Honour, about a third part of the way. We are passing the bog called Mona-Reulta."

"These savage Irish names of yours," said the other, "are very unmemorable." Though Lord Deputy of Ireland, he did not know one word of Gaelic, at a time when nearly every nobleman and gentleman in the island spoke, or could speak that tongue. "Tell me the meaning of it in English ; so I shall the better remember."

" Your Honour, it means the bog of stars, or starry bog. The bog is full of little pools and holes, and they show the stars most noticeably on a clear night."

" It is a singular name," remarked the other. He rode in silence for a while after that, and then added, " Master Edmund Spenser, my very ingenious friend, would be pleased to hear that name. Dost thou know, Tom, that this same ravaging monster and bird of prey whom we seek to-night is in the *Faery Queen*? The Ninth Canto of the Sixth Book is altogether conversant with him. Malengin is his name there. One Talus beat him full sore with his iron flail. Ay, Tom, the villain is in the *Faery Queen,* therefore famous for ever, rascal as he is. And I—alas !"

" I know not that, your Honour. I know he was in Idrone, yesterday was se'nnight, and drove the prey of thirteen towns, and murthered many loyal subjects. It is all a lie about Talus. There was no such captain, seneschal, or deputy in Ireland at any time."

The Deputy laughed cheerily at this sally, or whatever it may have been.

The army was now winding between high mountains, along a narrow way by the side of a rushing river, which roared loudly, swollen by the winter rains. Hour after hour the army pursued its march through wild mountain scenery now all hidden in

the folds of night. At length, after having climbed
one considerable eminence, the guide spoke some
words to the leader, and pointed down the valley.
The army halted. All the officers came together,
and conversed apart in low voices. In the valley
beneath lay the strong nest of that " proud bird
of the mountains " for whose extermination they
had come so far. Dawn was approaching. Already
the dense weight of the darkness was much relaxed.
They could see dimly the walls and towers of the
chieftain's stronghold, showing white in the surrounding dusk, or half-concealed by trees. It was
not a castle, only a small town, with walls and
gates.

Then cautiously the Lord Deputy's army began
to descend from the heights. Silence was enjoined
on all, not to be broken on pain of death. Each
subaltern was responsible for the behaviour of his
own file ; he had strict orders to keep his men together, and prevent straying on any pretext. As
they drew nearer, the scaling ladders were un-
packed. The little city as yet gave no sign of alarm ;
not a cock crowed or dog barked. No watch had
been set, or, if there had been, he slept. All within,
man and beast, seemed plunged in profound
slumber. Some strong detachments now separated
from the main body, and moved through the trees
to the right and the left. Their object was to sur-
round the city, and cut off all retreat. There was

another gate at the rear, opening upon a wooden bridge, which spanned a considerable stream. There were only two gates to the city, that in front, at which the main body was assembled, and the rear gate, whither the detachments were now tending. They never got there. At one moment there was silence, broken only by the murmuring of the stream or the occasional crackling of some trodden twig; at the next, the silence rang with the sharp, clear roll of a kettle-drum, the detonations so rapid that they seemed one continuous noise:—

> " Oh, listen, for the vale profound
> Is overflowing with the sound."

As suddenly as that drum had sounded, so abruptly it ceased; some one struck the drummer boy to the earth senseless, perhaps lifeless. But he had done his work. The roll of the kettle-drum can no more be recalled than the spoken word. The city, so sound asleep one minute past, was now awake and alive in every fibre. Bugles sounded there; arms and armour rang, and fierce voices in a strange tongue shouted passionate commands. Dogs bayed, horses neighed, women wailed, and children wept; and all the time the noise of trampling feet sounded like low thunder, a bass accompaniment to all that treble. The fume and glare of fast multiplying torches rose above the white walls, which were now alive with the morions of armed men, and presently ablaze with firearms. The assailants were themselves surprised and taken unawares. Their various detachments were separated. The original plan of assault had miscarried, and new arrangements were necessary. The leader bade his trumpeter sound the recall, and withdrew his men out of range, with the loss of a few wounded. When half-an-hour later a general attack was made on the walls, there was no one to receive it. They stormed an evacuated town. The chieftain, all his men, women, and children, all his animals, and the most valuable of his movable property, were seen dimly at the other side of the river, moving up the dark valley, with the men of war in the rear. Pursuit was dangerous, and was not attempted. The half-victorious army took half-joyful possession of the deserted city.

There was a court-martial a little before noon in the chieftain's feasting chamber, which was filled with armed men. A culprit was led before the Lord Deputy. His face was pale, and neck red with blood, and the hair on one side of his head wet and sticky. He was a well-formed, reddish-haired youth, blue-eyed, of features rather homely than handsome. It was the drummer. The court-martial did not last long. The evidence of the witnesses went straight home, and was not met or parried.

" Sirrah," cried the Lord Deputy, " why didst thou do it ? Why, being man to the Queen, didst thou play the traitor ? Gentlemen, what doth the lad say ?''

'' He says, an it please your Honour, that he could do nothing else ; that he saw this thing shine before him like a star.''

''Then is a traitor turned poet. Provost-marshal, take a file of snaphance-men, and shoot him off-hand. Nay, stay, a soldier's death is too good for him. Captain Lee, take him with thee in thy return, and drown him in that bog thou mindest of. Let him add that, his star, to the rest.''

Yet it was observed that the Lord Deputy remained silent for a while, and seemed to meditate ; after which he sighed and asked if there were another prisoner.

That evening a company of soldiers stood on a piece of firm ground above a dark pool in Mona-Reulta. They had amongst them a lad pinioned hand and foot, with a stone fastened to his ankles. He was perfectly still and composed ; there was even an expression of quiet pride in his illuminated countenance. He was to die a dog's death, but he had been true to his star. Two gigantic pike-men who had laid aside their defensive armour, but retained their helmets, raised him in their strong arms, while a third soldier simultaneously lifted the heavy stone. One, two, three, a splash, a rushing together in foam of the displaced water, then comparative stillness, while bubbles continually rose to

the surface and burst.   Presently all was still as
before, black and still.   One or two of the young
soldiers showed white scared faces ; but the mature
men, bearded English, and moustached Irish, sent
a hearty curse after the traitor, and strode away.
Soon the company stood ranked on the yellow road.
Someone gave out a sharp word of command, the
fifes struck up a lively measure, and all went cheerily
off at a quick march.   There was one horseman,
Captain Thomas Lee, a brave gentleman, honourably known in all the wars of the age.   Above them,
unrolled from the staff fluttered the bright folds of
their guidon.   The westering sun scintillated on their
polished armour and the bright points of their
pikes.   *They* were not traitors, but true men ; no
one could say that *they* had eaten the Queen's
rations, and handled her money only to betray her
cause.   Then the sound of the fifes died away in
the distance, and the silence of the uninhabited
wilderness resumed its ancient reign.   Faint breaths
of air played tenderly in the rushes and dry grass.
By-and-by a pert blackhead clambered about aim-
lessly in a little dry and stunted willow tree that
grew by the drummer's pool hardly a foot high.

Then the sun set, and still night increased, and
where the drummer boy had gone down a bright
star shone ; it was the evening star, the star of
love, which is also the morning star, the star of
hope and bravery.

PHILIP O'SULLIVAN:
HISTORIAN, SOLDIER AND POET.

IN the summer of 1602, a Spanish vessel of the kind known as a " patache," weighed anchor in the Kenmare River and sailed for Spain. She had been moored for a few days in front of the fine castle of Ardea. On the deck, weeping, stood a little boy of nine or ten years of age. His name was Philip; he was first cousin, once removed, of the Lord O'Sullivan, chief of the O'Sullivan nation and Prince of Beare and Bantry—the last independent dynast of those regions. The chieftain had rebelled against Queen Elizabeth, and, by the way of clearing the decks for action, had determined to send the children of the sept into Spain for safety; for in those days, Irish warfare did not spare children. The war, long repelled by the prowess of the chieftain, at last rolled in upon O'Sullivan's territory. At the moment O'Sullivan was barring the passes of Glengariffe against the advance of the Royalists, and there was desperate fighting every day in the " rough-glen."

The father of the little exile was lord of an island

called the Dorses, lying beyond the entrance of
Bantry Bay towards the west, and of some adjoining territory on the mainland. In this island Philip's
father had built himself a strong castle, and built
too a little church ; the ruins of both are still visible.
There were also the remains of an ancient monastery, long since sacked and destroyed "by pirates."
Here Philip was born. He was the youngest of
seventeen children, all born of the same parents.
The father of this extensive family was Dermot,
first cousin of the insurgent chieftain, a man who
has made his mark in history, being one of the
chief characters in that fine historical episode of
which some of my readers may have heard, "The
Retreat of the O'Sullivans." Philip, writing of his
island home, calls it Bea, but it is marked on the
map as Dorses, or Dursey Island. Pilgrimages will
yet be made to that island as the birthplace of Philip
the Historian.

The little boy was kindly taken in hand by certain
Spanish grandees, was supplied with tutors and
instructors, and, in short, educated with great care.
He was an apt and docile pupil, and celebrates by
name all the persons who were concerned in his
education, particularly a fellow-countryman of his
own named Synott, to whom he afterwards addressed many of his poems.

Philip was not long in his new home before he
was joined by great numbers of Irish retugees driven

out of Ireland by the success of the Queen's arms.
He was joined by his father and mother, by the
survivors of his seventeen brothers and sisters, by
the chieftain of the O'Sullivans, and a vast number
of broken and ruined gentlemen, hailing from all
parts of Ireland, members of nearly all the principal
families in the island, scarred, war-worn old
veterans, many of whom had been through the
whole of "The Nine Years' War," and were full
of war-anecdotes and reminiscences, and of startling
adventures by field and flood. Strolling and conversing through the squares of Madrid with his
younger friends, or silent, but with open eyes and
ears, in the company of his elders as they sat around
the fireside, or after dinner over their wine, talking
ceaselessly of the great Irish wars, Philip absorbed
all that conversation, and stored it away in a
singularly exact and retentive memory. As he grew
older, and began to be aware that he had a faculty
for   writing,   Philip   determined   to   be   the
historian and poet of these scarred veterans,
to do for them what they could not do for themselves.   Hence the great value of his work—
Historia Hiberniæ.   It was not written by a mere
student, painfully poring over tedious State papers
and mouldy archives, but by one who had conversed
for many years with all the principal actors of the
Irish war theatre, and who was, consequently,
almost an eye-witness of the scenes which he

describes, and knew personally many of the characters. So his History abounds in personal traits, hair-breadth escapes, perilous adventures, heroic achievements, vivid battle-scenes, clever repartees, and is, in fact, one of the liveliest and most entertaining histories ever written The question remains, is it true? To this I answer that it is certainly most veracious. Philip tells his stories exactly as he received them, and that his informants related the actual incidents, on the whole, with exactitude, we can see, by a comparison of Philip's stories with the same as told in the bald and hostile accounts scattered through the State Papers and taken down immediately after the events. The difference between Philip's stories and the State Papers' accounts resembles the difference between figures emblazoned on cathedral panes seen from *within* the building and the same seen from *without,* the difference between grey clouds and the same steeped in sunset hues. The difference, in fact, lies for the most part in colour and suggestion. Again Philip makes the very natural mistake that his heroes were champions of the Catholic religion. As such they received great honour in Spain and noble pensions from the Spanish king. They in fact, were not mainly concerned about religion. What they generally fought for was their rights and privileges as feudal lords. This gives an ecclesiastical flavour to Philip's History. Its chief value

lies in the curious and suggestive details with which
it abounds. Here is just one example. After de-
scribing the battle of the Blackwater in his own
lively and vigorous style, Philip tells how a certain
General Romley pursued by Tyrone's horse, and
finding flight hopeless, quietly sat down by the side
of the road, drew forth his pipe and tobacco-box,
and smoked up to the moment of his death. He was
slain while absorbing the smoke of tobacco through
a tube. The whole history abounds in such charming
and suggestive touches. Philip, as he grew up,
was undetermined whether to devote himself to war
or to the Muses. He finally resolved to culti-
vate both, like Cervantes, Raleigh, Sydney,
and many other famous soldier-writers of that age.
He fought duels too; one of them—a most disastrous affair—he describes himself. A Norman-
Irish gentleman named Batty conversing with
Philip's chief, The O'Sullivan, threw out some
reflection upon the dignity of that family. Philip
who was present, said not a word but went out,
waited for the contumelious man and *expostulated*
with him. Result—drawn swords. The chieftain
hastened out to put an end to the duel, but in doing
so got his death wound, not from Philip, but
from Batty. The likeness of that chieftain,
Donal O'Sullivan, *Comes de Bearra,* painted in
Madrid will be found in our National Gallery
in the Leinster Lawn. Philip entered the service

of the Spanish King as a soldier. Whether
he distinguished himself as such I cannot tell, but
he was very likely to have done so. Besides his
History he wrote many Latin poems in elegiac
verse. Philip O'Sullivan's *Historia Hiberniæ* is
one of the best literary monuments of Ireland.

KIEGANGAIR.

INTRODUCTION.

The following story relates the cause of a small rebellion
by which the Government was much annoyed in 1588, and
several succeeding years. Through this story as through
a small window, one can see something of a very singular
state of society. The narrator is one of the servants of the
insurgent Macanerla, a title which means Son of the Earl.
It must be remembered that in those days there surrounded
Earls, too, something of the divinity that hedged a King.

CHAPTER I.

THE BILLETING OF KIEGANGAIR.

WE, the people of Donald M'Cartie, the Earl's
only son, were all together in the great hall of his
castle, awaiting the arrival of the Queen's messenger who was to fetch away our lord to London for
conference with Elizabeth and the Council. Now,
my lord Donald was a man of power over all
M'Cartie More's country, and the Queen and
Council desired to confer with him, so as to secure
good order there under the circumstances set forth,
the people being at the time without any rightful
chief, lord, captain or earl.

We had our best plate out that night, so that
the board shone with silver, and the hall, too, was

all draped, and we wore each man his bravest
raiment and ornaments in honour of the Queen, and
also in honour of the messenger, for he was chief of
the nation of the Prestons—i.e., that sept of them
which was known as the " proud Prestons " of
Lancaster. My lord's mother was of the Irish
branch. My lord stood before the fire, which was
at the end of the hall, and his favourite hound
Kiegangair stood up against him, resting his fore-
paws on his shoulders, while my lord held the dog's
head between his hands. I often saw them stand
so before, and now recall it to mind clear as a
picture, for it was the last time that they stood
together so. Without it was a wild night, all darkness, wind, and rain. Then we heard the clattering
of hoofs, and the noise of a troop in the courtyard.

The Preston, when he arrived, was a surprise to
us, for he was young and pleasant-looking, like
The Macanerla, and gay of speech and laughter-
loving.

You would have thought that he and The
Macanerla were brothers, save that my lord was
fair-haired and somewhat older. They sat together
at the end of the table, and many times my lord
pledged him, and drank to the health of the house
of Preston—both the English branch and the Irish.
Three barrels of red wine of Rochelles were
broached that night.

At last The Macanerla rose and led his guest

with him into a withdrawing room, that they might talk together more privately. The hound rose at the same time and followed his master into the other room. There he lay down upon the hearth, and relaxed his strong limbs in sleep. Tawny orange was his hue, and he wore round his neck a collar of fine silver. That night I was in personal attendance on the lord.

My lord and young Preston read together the Lord Burleigh's letter, or rather Preston read it, my lord listening and looking over his shoulder, and they conversed together at first gravely, but after that more hilariously, and often they pledged each other, either wishing the other good fortune. There was no light in the chamber, save the blazing logs and turf on the hearth, which it was my duty to replenish, and beside which the great hound lay outstretched. Without, the storm grew fiercer, the wind wheezed and coughed in the wide chimney, from time to time heavy raindrops fell and hissed upon the red brands.

My lord and his guest paused in their conversation, and contemplated the hound, for he moaned in his slumbers, and, as dreaming dogs will, worked with his forefeet and scattered the ashes on the hearth. He started to his feet, while the hairs on his back erected themselves, and charged across the chamber, and standing at the door bayed savagely a deep note of warning and of rage. The

Macanerla laughed. He called the dog back, and caressing him, said, " No, Kiegangair, it was but a dream. It is not as it used to be!" Then, turning to his guest, he said, " You would not be surprised at our friendship if you knew what we suffered together, I and Kiegangair. Once being wronged, I went into action of rebellion, drawing along with me a large party of my own clan and others, and for a while defended the action successfully. Then one mischance followed another, and of my comrades some were slain and some taken prisoner, and others, despairing, fled the country, and some, turning traitors for reward, had dealings with the President and Council that they might betray me. In the end, I was forsaken of all, and being under the ban of outlawry, was chased to and fro. But, O Kiegangair, thou wouldst not forsake me! When I slept, whether in cave or tree or under the ground, he mounted guard, a faithful and vigilant sentry, and ever awoke me when there was the smallest suspicion of danger. Before me, as I fled, he went exploring thickets and marshes, searching for parties in ambush, of which were many. Armed men he has dragged down fighting by my side. Also thou were my food-provider, Kiegangair, when we hunted not for sport, but that we might remain alive. Often we fasted and spent sleepless nights, lying close together for warmth, when famine would not suffer us to sleep. Once when I had a fever, he nursed me, bringing me water in my helmet from the stream. Yea, Kiegangair, we have suffered many things together when all the world was against us." The Macanerla bowed his yellow head low, caressing the hound, while tears sprung from his eyes as he thought of all the sorrows of the past, and the love and courage of his matchless hound. " The morning with its full light would come upon us," he said, " ere I could make an end of telling even a tithe of the things which Kiegangair and I have suffered and done in each other's company, when we were outlaws."

The Macanerla and the young Saxon gentleman, his cousin, slept that night in the same bed, and kissed each other ere they slept. Early in the morning The Macanerla called his chief officers, and bade them quarter all his soldiers, horse and foot, and his dogs and dog-boys, and hawks and hawk-boys upon the gentleman of Cork and Desmond till his return. He bade his master of the hounds quarter Kiegangair upon a certain Shane Du, a rich farmer in Desmond, and tenant to a small lord there named O'Falvey. The morning was bright and fine. It was October, and the woods all ruddy and russet, and bright gold ; a calm had succeeded the storm, and there was hoar frost on the ground and on the leaves. The sun too rose clear and strong and all the world looked

happy. The Macanerla took an affectionate farewell of Kiegangair, and the boy who had charge of
him led him away into the O'Falvey's country, in
Desmond of deep valleys.

CHAPTER II.

FUN BY THE WAYSIDE

As soon as we had broken our fast we got to horse
in order to accompany our lord to Cork, where he
was to embark for Barstable and we rode down the
Lee Valley. My lord and Preston rode together.
Plumes danced, bright capes and mantles fluttered,
and chain reins rang pleasantly that morning.

Then, as ill-luck would have it, we riding to
Cork after the Earl's son, met O'Falvey riding from
Cork into Desmond. Where we met, the road was
lifted up like a causeway, and on our left side between the road and the fence there was a deep gut
filled with water, owing to the heavy rain of the
previous night. O'Falvey who was weighty and
stout, rode upon a powerful hackney. His two
servants were also well mounted, and three horse
boys ran beside the horses. The two servants
saluted the Macanerla respectfully. O'Falvey did
not salute at all, but looked fixedly before him. I

noted his eyes as I passed, and they were filled
with pride, anger, and rebellion. My lord did not
observe that affront. We who did said to one
another, " This churl standeth on his charter. He
is a no man's man forsooth."

After we who were beside or behind The
Macanerla had passed by, the main body of our
troop came up, and certain of the younger men
stopped O'Falvey and demanded of him why he
had not capped the Earl's son, and O'Falvey
answered stiffly, " Cap him yourselves ; he is no
lord of mine " ; and they answered, " Nay, but he
is thy lord ; for time out of mind the O'Falvies have
been followers to M'Cartie More, and if he were
not thy lord yet is he an Earl's son, and to be
capped by one like thee." It was Garret Mac
Randal O'Leary, of Sweet Prospect, who said this,
and as he said it he drove his horse, which was a
chief horse, or horse of war, alongside of
O'Falvey's. And first he made the chief horse
push O'Falvey's beast playfully with his hind-
quarters, and then to butt at him playfully with his
foreshoulder, and so, while he (Garret) still voci-
ferated, and O'Falvey responded with counter-
vociferation, in the end he pushed the other and his
horse clean off the highway, so that both fell into
the gripe. Then our young men raised a great
shout of joyous laughter, and rode swiftly after
their lord. and the event supplied them with much

mirthful conversation for the rest of the way.
Moreover, they composed a song upon that theme
with an appropriate chorus, and chanted it as they
rode, singing with open mouths the discomfiture
of O'Falvey, and ironically praising the war-
prowess of Garret, son of Randal. So spent, the
time was not long ere the east gate of Cork, adorned
with many heads, rose to view.

CHAPTER III.

O'FALVEY'S REVENGE

MEANTIME O'Falvey, assisted by his servants,
climbed with difficulty out of the gripe, and muddy
and dripping, remounted his horse, and rode home-
ward silent. He was devoured by anger and
hatred. When he reached home his people came
out into the yard to meet him, bearing torches.
Then when the light fell upon his features, which
were dry and aggravated, the word went round
amongst them that the lord was not at ease in his
mind.

O'Falvey, after he had changed his clothes and
supped and had drunk somewhat, broke the silence
by asking his chief steward for the news.

The steward answered : " There is no news
other than that a dog and a dog boy of The

Macanerla have arrived this day, and taken quarters with Shane Du, of Glasnafinshon,"—viz., the Torrent of the Ash trees.

O'Falvey bade the steward kill the dog early the next morning, and beat the dog boy over the mearing. "The Queen," he said, "will bear me through in that action."

But the steward made answer clear and bold that he would not hurt a hair of the head of either of them, of the dog or the boy.

"Thou art afraid," said O'Falvey.

"Afraid or not," said the steward, "I will not do it. Do it yourself."

"I will," said O'Falvey.

"Have a care, my lord," said his wife, who sat next to him at the right. "Have a care I beseech thee, for I think the dog is Kiegangair."

"Who has seen the dog?" said the chief.

"I saw him, your honour," answered a boy who with others sat at the supper table. "His colour is yellow-red, one colour throughout, without spot or stripe; his head is small, considering his great size, and for beauty there is not his like in Desmond. A young gentleman, bravely attired, led him by a chain of polished brass fastened to a collar of silver. A laden garran, attended by a churl, was with him. I saw the party in the bohareen that leads down to the torrent where are the falls. They stood awhile all together, looking at the white falls. My lord, the dog is Kiegangair."

O'Falvey smiled to himself, but said nothing. He perceived that his people by no means approved of the ill deed which he meditated. After supper he and the lady went into a private room. There with dried leaves of tobacco tree he filled the bowl of a long earthen pipe, and after he had ignited and inflamed it he silently inhaled the noisome smoke into his lungs and vitals, and again expelled it in blue rolling volumes both from his nostrils and his mouth. This was a common practice with O'Falvey, whensoever he might take food, whether in the morning or at midday or at night. He was slovenly in attire, and wore an Abraham's beard.

His wife sat apart and plied her needle embroidering a garment for her son. His cradle was by her side, and she wrought having one foot on the rocker. This night a great fear gathered like ice around her heart, and shapeless terror beat the air with unseen wings. She was of the Geraldines of the West—viz., a fair bud of the stem of Raymond the Conqueror, and was famous in all Desmond for beauty, hospitality, good counsel, and elegant manners.

" The Macanerla is gone into England," she said.

" That he may stay there !" said O'Falvey.

" That would be a gallant gentleman lost to us,"

she answered, "and a good friend to thee and me."

"He quarters his dogs and dog boys on us and devours our living," quoth the chief.

"Nay, my lord," she said, "some ill counsellor hath spoken with thee; see, The Macanerla has entrusted to us his favourite and much-loved hound, Kiegangair, whose fame is noised over the five provinces for courage and faithfulness. He sent thee but one dog, and that dog was Kiegangair."

So far she spoke, and then kept silence.

When O'Falvey had made an end of that monstrous and astonishing fumigation of his internal parts he began to drink, and as the drink inflamed him his wrath against The Macanerla and the whole breed and seed of great lords grew hotter. Then he arose and left the house by a postern, avoiding the great hall where were his people, and went in the direction of a light which was further down in the valley, steering his course by that bad star. It was an alehouse, to which the churls and rude rustical people of the vicinity used to resort, and whose society he preferred to that of his own household. They were glad when they saw him, and stood up, but he bade them resume their seats. To these ignoble folk then he related the insults and oppressions of The Macanerla, and they fed his humour and flattered him to his ruin. He slept there that night, and in the morning, attended by a great crowd of plebeian folk, his tenants, he went on to the valley of the Stream of the Ash Trees to the house of Shane Du. As they approached the house Kiegangair and the dog boy came out together, followed by Shane Du. The dog boy was a lad of some twenty years, with the first down on his unrazored lip, very comely, and a dear friend to The Macanerla. He wore a doublet of green velvet and a little scarlet cape, and had two long darts in his left hand. His right rested on the head of Kiegangair.

Kiegangair, seeing the multitude of plebeians, growled low and fierce, for he was wont to associate only with men of war and gentlemen; but when O'Falvey drew nigh, not perceiving in his simplicity what lay underneath the buff coat and plumed hat, nor what a churl was girded with a sword, the dog approached him with an air of welcome. Then O'Falvey drew his sword and ran it twice through the body of Kiegangair, and as the boy ran forward, he was seized by strong rustic arms and hurled to the ground, and his head struck against the stone seat which was under the eaves of the house by the door, and he became insensible.

Shane Du the while stood in the doorway, his face white upon the darkness behind. He did not stir, though indignant, fearing to make bad worse.

Kiegangair, collapsing in a lake of blood, moaned a little, was silent, and gazed at his murderer.

O'Falvey thought to run him through the third
time, but was afraid.

Then the wretched man went home, boasting
as he went, but there was no heart in his boasting.
His people dropped away from him one by one, so
that he entered his house alone.   When she saw
him, his wife cried—"Thou hast killed Kiegangair.
Thou hast slain innocence and truth.   God will
requite thee for that evil deed !"

And the chief answered—" It was no evil deed.
Listen, O woman ! for I shall convict thee of folly.
I was in the great hall of the Royal fortress of
Shandon, and one of the gentlemen of the Lee
Valley asked Sir John Perrott what he should do
when a great lord sent in dogs and dog boys to be
quartered upon him.   And Sir John Perrott
stamped with his foot, so, and answered—' 'S
death, man !   Kill the dogs and scourge the dog
boys over the mearings. These dotish old customs,'
said he, ' are ended ; know that, once for all.   If
the great lords break their charters, I will break
them.   That I swear.'   Those were his very words,
and he said them in the hearing of the White
Knight, and Patrick Condon, and the three
M'Carties."

Never before had O'Falvey spoken so long or so
well.   His wife was silent for a while, and then she
said—" Show me thy charter," and when he gave

it to her she drew a scissors from a little scabbard in her girdle, and thrust it through the document.

" See," she said, " what goes through it, and driven by what a hand ! Man, it is but parchment."

CHAPTER IV.

THE MACANERLA'S RETURN.

WHEN The Macanerla returned to Ireland in December, many of us, his people, rode to Moyallo to meet him. As we drew towards home The Macanerla halted at a rising ground near the castle, and said : —

" Hark, now we shall hear the grand baying of Kiegangair."

He was surprised and disappointed that he did not. When we rode into the courtyard, and the other hounds came round him, he called aloud for Kiegangair. The master of the hounds said that Kiegangair was not yet arrived. The Macanerla said : —

" Is he well ?" and the master answered, " He is well," but his face blenched as he said it, and when the lord turned away he made upon himself the sign of the cross, as if that could wipe away the stain of the untruth.

" To-morrow," said The Macanerla, " we will draw the woods of Ballyvourney for a pig—there is a lusty one there—but not until Kiegangair arrives. Send a horseman to quicken the movements of the slow boy."

As he entered the castle he paused with one foot on the threshold and said :—

" I hear a moaning as of a sick hound." A second lie was told when he said that, so that shame and horror fell upon us who heard it. We thought that it would not be so bad as by actual proof we now found it to be.

At supper The Macanerla was very gay, and related many things concerning London, and the great people and sights there, and concerning the respect with which he had been treated by the lords of the Council and the Queen.

" Dear friends and comrades," he said, " I am right glad to be at home once more ; would that Kiegangair were here ; then would my happiness be complete."

When he said this there entered the hall a youth bearing a dog in his arms. It was Kiegangair, swathed and bandaged, still alive, and reaching forth his neck to come to his dear master. He had just sufficient strength to lick once more for the last time his dear master's face, then his head fell forward, and the brave spirit went out of him and he died. When The Macanerla stood silent and bewildered, the lad spoke.

" O Macanerla ! " he said, " they bade me conceal all till to-morrow, that thou mightest have thy first night happy in the courts of thy fathers and amongst thy dear comrades. But when Kiegangair was dying, and because he knew thy voice, I said I would bring him to thee, that you might look on one another once more ere the black river roll between. And it is not by the act of God he is dead before thee, but by the devisings of the devil and the hand of a bad chief, for it was O'Falvey who slew him, who stabbed him twice because he was thy dog, and because he was quartered upon him, he said, unlawfully."

Then Donald Bwee, the rigdamna, or heir apparent of the Clan Cartie, high and puissant lifted up his voice and cried aloud for his dog, even as a young man laments for his dear friend and comrade whom he loves more than life, so The Macanerla without shame and without restraint, cried aloud, for the flood-tide of his grief, strong and impetuous, could not be controlled ; and the women in the castle and in all the town round about when they heard him, lifted up their voices too and raised the cry of the dead, for the great sorrow of the young lord overflowed into all hearts. After that the Earl's son drew forward the folds of his mantle of fine scarlet lined with ermine, and concealed in them his face, bowing low his noble head, and his eyes became like rivers and his mantle was steeped in tears, and no word came from his mouth till a third part of the night was spent, and all his people sat in silence on account of his sorrow. They extinguished the lights and neither ate nor drank. Then in the middle of the night at first cock crow The Macanerla stood up, and speaking to us with a voice hoarse and untuned, he said that he would exact a terrible and long-remembered retribution on the murderers of Kiegangair, and when we said that we would bear him out in that course, aye, though it brought him into action of rebellion against the English queen, he bade the bugle sound " to horse." By the light of torches our horses were accoutred. Many hours we rode darkling, moving ever northwards into Desmond up the valley of the Black Allo, following the white plume of our lord ; and the dawn broke cold and grey. When we came into O'Falvey's country it was silent and empty. Marvelling at that we rode on to the chief's mansion, which was in a sheltered valley, having its back to the north wind. We thought at first that it too was empty, but when we came close to it we saw a man sitting in an upper window, and knew that it was O'Falvey. When we challenged him he came out at once, descending on the out-side by a ladder. How he came to be there I learned afterwards from himself. It happened in this way.

When O'Falvey heard that The Macanerla was
about to return home he went to Sir Warham St.
Leger, and required of him an army for his defence.

Sir Warham said:—" I cannot give thee an
army, but this I surely promise, that when The
Macanerla kills thee I will be in no haste to forgive
him."

With this mock sounding in his ear O'Falvey
returned to Desmond. That night he had evil
dreams—viz., Kiegangair, grown to giant size,
hunting him over land and sea, and he awoke and
feared to sleep again. The next day he made preparations for the removal of all his people, and the
complete evacuation of his territory, and again at
night had bad dreams, and the following day they
set out and escaped into the country of the Knight
of the Valley. But thither he said Kiegangair
pursued him in visions of the night, and then in
broad daylight, and with his waking eyes he saw
him, so that whether he waked or slept he could
get no ease. Accordingly one night, telling no one,
he mounted his horse and rode home. All the doors
having been made fast, it was by a ladder that he
entered his house. This was how he came to be
sitting in that window, for he expected our coming,
and the window commanded a good outlook down
the valley. While he sat there he recalled the words
of his father, " Stand ever by the Queen, my sons,
it is the post of honour and the post of safety." He

marvelled how it had become for him the post of
dishonour and early death. When my lord asked him
whether he had any defence or justification he
answered with a Saxon proverb which signifies
that when anything needs mending it will be soonest
repaired by keeping silence. He also said that he
did the deed contrary to the wish of his household
and the advisement of his wife. We bound him and
set him on a led horse, and brought him away. I
was appointed to minister to him, and when we
came home I gave him breakfast with strong ale
and a reasonable proportion of *aqua vitæ,* and he
ate and drank and smoked. He said that he was
happy in his mind, and while he smoked he
related many things to me, and amongst others how
he had spent his early manhood as supercargo of
merchant ships plying between Bristol and Havre,
and that he succeeded to his father's place by an
accident.

" When I resolved to give myself up," he said,
" the dog ceased to haunt me."

He would have no priest to visit him, but he
repeated a prayer in the Saxon tongue, and the
names of his wife and of his little son were frequent
in that prayer. The same day we buried Kiegangair
under a tree on the west side of the castle near the
river, and there we hanged O'Falvey on the same
tree. Then the Earl's son and all we his people,
bathed and changed our clothes and we entered the

great hall and lit many candles, and ate and drank, and the Earl's son spoke comfortably about Kiegangair, and related certain of his feats. He said he would exact no further eric on the clan of O'Falvey, but would, if anything, rather make amends to the widow and the innocent child. Shortly after he said this, word was brought to him that a party of O'Falvey's people were without and begged the body of their lord. The Macanerla ordered it to be given to them, and also horses and the best car in the town for the conveyance of the body, and that for their piety and faithfulness they should be hospitably treated by his servants. Accordingly, when they had eaten and drunk to their satisfaction, they cut down the body and took it away with them into Desmond and made lamentation over the slain man and recounted his good deeds.

The President sent a troop to arrest The Macanerla for the murder, and they returned saying that they were not strong enough. Then he sent against him an army under the command of Captain Bostock. The Macanerla retreated into the west of the country into Desmond, stood upon his keeping for a long time after that, and was proclaimed as a rebel against his sovereign.

THE
VENGEANCE OF THE O'HAGANS.

" I'll tell thee a story
And a story that's true."

(Old Song.)

The following story supplies a picture of wild feudal Irish
life in the 16th century outside the precincts of the Pale and
the regions directly governed by the Viceroy of Ireland and
the Council.

CHAPTER I.

A GENTLEMAN OF ULSTER.

In the time of the Great Earl of Tyrone, and before
he went into rebellion against Her Highness the
Queen, there was a gentleman of the Earl's clan
named Felim O'Neill, whose chief house was upon
an island in the midst of a small lake close to the
Bann. A bridge of timber ran from the mainland
to the island at the point where the lake was
narrowest. It was protected by a fort at the end
where it touched the mainland. The bridge was
movable, and could be let up or down, like the
drawbridge of a moat. There was a strong wall

surrounding the island protected with stakes and palisades. When Felim's people at night drew up the drawbridge it became a portion of the wall. Within the island was the house of the lord. There was a lawn in front of the house, and, hard by, gardens and an orchard ; also ornamental timber. The house itself was low and thatched and built in the form of a square surrounding a courtyard, and the walls were white with lime. Felim had large estates and many tenants. He was a man of great power and wealth, but was under the government of the Earl, and paid him a customary rent.

One morning, as he sat at breakfast with his people, Felim addressed them all and said : — "The morning promises a fine day : let us ride to the north-western angle of my country," indicating it by name, " and bring with us one eyrie of our hawks. We shall have good sport and compel good entertainment, for I hear grouse are numerous in these townlands, and I know that the tenants have not paid me rent for a long time. If we cannot get money out of those churls, let us quarter ourselves upon them for a night and two days. They are too rich for churls. I promise they will not be too rich when we take our departure." He laughed pleasantly as he spoke, and his men laughed too.

CHAPTER II.

ON THE HIGH ROAD.

FELIM'S people were glad of that proposal, and made ready accordingly. The morning was, indeed, bright and fine, but the wind was high and made a curl upon the waters of the lake. When the hounds heard the noises of preparation and the trampling of the horses' hoofs upon the hollow-sounding causeway they bayed from their kennels. "That is a mournful noise which the hounds make to-day," said Felim. "Hark, how the Music-master wails! Is there anyone dead in the crannog, or in the town?"

"There is not, my lord," said one of his gentlemen; "but there may be before the day is done."

"It is an unpleasant sound," said Felim.

After that they all rode westward with the hawks, and what with the motion and noise of the horses and the ringing of the chain-reins, the jingling of spurs and the clanking of swords, and owing to the freshness of the morning, and their anticipations of good sport and agreeable night quarters, the whole company became very joyous, and they talked much and laughed as they went, and they went swiftly.

They were about ten miles from the crannog, and had but a little passed a place where two roads met when they saw far away a small company riding to meet them. At first they could not distinguish who they were, for they saw only the bright and various-coloured mantles fluttering in the wind, and one white plume as it were dancing in the midst of that company.

As they drew nearer one of Felim's people who was very sharp-sighted said : " The youth with the feather is Shane O'Hagan. Well, I know the saucy carriage of his head. That youth is the proudest limb of the small proud clans in Ireland to-day. Since their foster-brother the Earl has grown so great, they think no more of us all than if we were the pit gravel of the road under the feet of their horses."

CHAPTER III.

FELIM MUST FLY.

THEN one of Felim's chief men, whose name was Donnell Ogue, said, " That is the man who insulted thee at Castle Roe, on the Bann side," referring to something said or done by the youth, —said or done in boyish heedlessness and levity and straightway forgotten.

So the two companies, the great and the small, continually approaching, drew together. When

they came within speaking distance Shane
O'Hagan lifted up a loud clear friendly voice and
saluted Felim and his company. That Shane was a
very comely young man, blue eyed and yellow-
haired, and with the hair of early manhood just
showing on his upper lip. He was greatly beloved
by his brothers, and also by the Earl and the whole
of his own clan. Felim did not once raise his cap to
that salutation, or utter one word of a reply. Seeing
this the young man reddened, and the blush of
wrath and shame overspread his white forehead,
and, with a strong voice, he bade one of Felim's
people clear the road, and give free passage to the
foster-brethren of O'Neill—i.e., the Great Earl
high and mighty who was the head and captain of
Ulster in his day. All the particulars of what then
took place are not recorded, only that Felim's
people being many, drew upon that company being
few, and did not finish with them before they slew
that brave and dear youth, and also one faithful
follower, and put the rest to flight ; and that Felim
stood by, and never once interfered, by word or
act, while that cowardly slaughter was being committed. Then some of Felim's people were for
stripping the dead, as though they had been slain
in battle, and for seizing and making prey of their
horses ; but Felim with menacing words restrained
them, and he bade them restore Shane's sword to
his scabbard, for it had fallen from his grasp in the

fight. So they rode forward, Felim's men exulting and triumphant at having slain an enemy and avenged an insult to their dear lord and master; but Felim himself rode with a dark brow, and in silence, for when the first anger went out of him he repented, and bitterly he foresaw that the Earl or the kindred of the slain man would exact upon him a dreadful vengeance on account of that bad deed. So when they came to the next parting of the ways, the lord Felim said with a strong oath, that he would not go a-hawking or a-coshering that day, and he turned aside his horse's head and rode home by another way, so that he should not pass by the bodies, and all his people rode after him in silence. Sorrowful and anxious were their minds upon that return journey to the crannog. The sky, too, became gloomy and overcast with clouds, and the wind rose, so that when they reached the crannog, the lake was white with foam, and the black trees were violently agitated by the blast. Felim's people in the crannog were surprised at that early and unexpected return; and when she heard the noise of the horses' hoofs upon the bridge, his wife, Julia, daughter of the lord of Clannaboy, cast around her a mantle with a hood to cover the head, hastily, and came down to the bridge to meet him, for her mind misgave her that some mischief was abroad. She took with her her eldest son, Hugh, who was six years old lacking a month. When

Felim saw her he lighted down from his horse, and he kissed his little son. Then he walked with his wife alone to the house, and conversed with her for a long time in a private chamber. The resolution at which they arrived in that conference was, that Felim should ride at once to Dublin to the Lord Deputy and Council, bringing rich gifts, in order that they might make his peace with the Clan O'Hagan, and with the Earl. It was also resolved that the lady and the children should leave the crannog at the same time, and go to her father into the country of the children of Yellow Hugh— namely, Clannaboy. Felim also gave orders to his chief men to take away all the cattle and horses, flocks and herds, and movable property in general, for he greatly feared the wrath of the kindred of the slain man. These things were done, and Felim with Donnell Ogue—viz., the man who had that morning reminded him of the insult, and two others, taking to themselves fresh horses from the crannog.

CHAPTER IV.

CHRISTIAN MEEKNESS OF THE O'HAGANS.

THOSE who had escaped from that slaughter made by Felim and his people on the highway, galloped thence by a direct road to the place where were the brethren of the slain man. They happened at the time to be teaching the art of war to their young warriors. Some of these in doubtlets of scarlet and with battle-caps of brass upon their heads, were shooting out of calyvers, and others, dressed in Irish fashion, were casting their spears at a figure made of wood that stood a long way off ; and Hugh Ogue O'Hagan, the youngest brother of the murdered lad, was teaching them, for he was very expert in that art. The fugitives having related what was done, there broke forth from the assembly a great shout of wrath and sorrow, and the women who were in the castle and in the surrounding houses, when they heard them, lifted up their voices too, and the whole town was filled with lamentation.

But the eldest brother whose name was Owen, wept not nor lamented, nor did he utter one angry word, but kept his countenance with a powerful movement of the will, as though his features had been carved out of hard rock. He first ordered his constable to take and confine those fugitives, for he said that it was they who, by their cowardice, had slain his brother. Then he called to him his two surviving brothers—namely, Henry, skilful in the training of chief-horses, and Hugh Ogue, the expert hurler of spears, and bade them cease from their vain lamentation and weeping. When these had made an end of their mourning, the three brothers conferred together alone by themselves.

Afterwards, coming forth, Owen bade the horse-
boys get ready as many horses of service, and
hackneys, as were in the castle stables, or in the
town, and all the O'Hagans, as many as were
horsemen, armed themselves and put on their battle
dresses. So Owen O'Hagan took the road with a
score and two horsemen, and every man in a shirt
of ring mail, with his hauberk on his breast, and his
horseman's staff in his hand.

Soon they reached the scene of the slaughter,
which was easily distinguishable, for the road was
torn up from the trampling of the horses, and was
scattered with blood. The bodies, however, were
not immediately visible, for pious neighbours, poor
herdsmen and tillers of earth, who dwelt there, had
cast mantles upon them. On the road lay the body
of the servant, and on the roadside, where he fell,
lay the body of Shane. The road here was a tochar
or raised causeway, crossing a bog. When the boy
Shane got his death-blow, he had fallen from his
horse on the edge of the tochar, and thence rolled
over into the bog, but his plumed hat was caught
in a thorn that grew on the edge of the way, and
the body lay underneath that thorn in the bog, for
no one dared touch or remove it till the kindred had
arrived. There were four cailleachs (old women)
beating their hands together as they swayed to and
fro, and making great lamentation over the body.
On the road were certain churls holding the horses

of the slain men: When Owen raised the mantle
that covered the face of his dear brother, and when
they all recognised the features of their kinsmen,
they wept anew and lamented, but Owen neither
lamented nor wept. He inquired of the country
people whether they had any news from the crannog, and when they told him that the lord had
departed one way and the lady another, " That is
well," he said. " Enough blood has been spilled
this day."

They made two litters with their horsemen's
staves for the bearing of the bodies, and cast over
them the costliest and most beautiful mantles in all
the company, and having rewarded the mourning-
women, as was right, they returned along the road
that they had come. After the obsequies many
persons, both kindred and friends, spoke with Owen
and his brothers about taking vengeance for that
deed ; but still he kept saying that enough of blood
had been spilled over the quarrel, that sharp tongues
draw on sharp swords, that it was the Earl's
business, and other such like speeches. Though
the crannog was empty and deserted they never
went there. A report of the mild speeches and
demeanour of the three brethren went abroad over
the country, and some men praised and some men
blamed.

Then Felim's people whom he had left in Ulster,
and who were weary of living upon the hospitality

of strangers and foreigners, took courage and ventured home. They were under the leading of Felim's younger brother, and they came back with their flocks and herds and horses and movables, and occupied the crannog again, and all the rich demesne lands of Lord Felim. But they made themselves as strong as they could against the O'Hagans and kept good watch and ward. Yet, was the demeanour of the O'Hagans towards them quiet and peaceable. They uttered no angry speech and did not touch corn nor horn on all Felim's estates.

CHAPTER V.

PERQUISITES OF OFFICE.

FELIM and Donnell Ogue rode straight from the crannog to Dublin. They took lodgings in a street near the Castle, and by the advice of Sir Henry Bagenal, Marshal of Ireland, they sent rich gifts to the Lord Deputy Fitzwilliam and to the Council. The Lord Deputy sent for Felim, and received him in a private chamber of the Castle. He was under physic at the time, being of a moist constitution of body. Moreover he suffered sorely from gout. His foot which was swathed in warm flannels, was resting upon a stool curiously embroidered, when Felim entered that sumptuous apartment and made his reverence to the Chief Governor of Ireland. Fitzwilliam nevertheless pointed out to Felim the great heinousness of his offence and the disgrace it would be to the Queen's Government if due punishment were not inflicted for that slaying of the young man Shane O'Hagan. Felim returned sadly to his lodgings, but after further conference with the Marshal he sent more and richer gifts to the Lord Deputy, and promised besides that he would send to him the two casts of falcons which he had left behind in the crannog if haply they had not been already seized by the O'Hagans or by the great Earl. Felim advanced in the good opinions of the Lord Deputy and Council after that. Subsequently the great Earl came to Dublin. The Lord Deputy and Council spoke to him about that matter of Felim, and ordered him to pardon Felim. The Earl was much displeased at being obliged to pardon a man who, while under his own government, had murdered his foster-brother. They also ordered him to treat Felim in every respect like the rest of his freehold tenants, and in the third place to forgive him a year's rent. These were hard conditions to impose upon a man like him. Felim's gifts accordingly brought in a good return. They also drew out a solemn pardon of their own for Felim and signed it, and it was sealed with the Seal of the Realm, and it was placed in the Archives of the State, and it is there now. All this of course was a great indignity to the Earl, but he feared that he would not be allowed to depart on this occasion but that he would be taken prisoner and sent to England, and there destroyed after the manner of Sir John Perrott. He did what he was required, yet he stated openly to the Council that it was not in his power to defend Felim after what he had done, and that Felim would surely come to an ill end if he again went down to Ulster relying on these pardons and promises.

Felim, accordingly, still feared to return home, but in the end, though he mistrusted the mild speeches of the O'Hagans which were reported to him, he felt sad and unhappy at being such a long time away from his country. So he rode down again to Ulster, and came first to the country of the children of Yellow Hugh—viz., the O'Neills of Clannaboy, his wife's people, and there his wife advised him to go straight to the Earl wherever he might be, and ask him to take their eldest child Hugh to foster. She said that if the Earl would consent and entered the sacred bonds of fosterage with them, then they might all safely return to the crannog; but that if the Earl refused they had best never go back any more. She also told him that he should keep well on his guard against the brothers of the slain man and not to trust himself with the O'Hagans anywhere save under the eyes of the Earl, and not even there if he could help it.

CHAPTER VI.

FELIM VISITS THE EARL.

FELIM, accordingly, took to him Donnell Ogue, who had been with him from the first, though he had been but an ill friend to him, and Heber O'Neill, son of Rory, and Calvach O'Neill, son of Ferdoragh, and others the most valiant of the gentlemen who were his kindred, and crossed the mearings and entered Tyrone. There having made enquiries he learned that the Earl was encamped, above all other places, at Felim's own crannog. His informant also told him that the Earl's forces occupied tents which they had pitched round about the lake, and that the Earl and the Countess, Mabel Bagenal, daughter of the Marshal, were in the house upon the island, and that Hugh Maguire, Lord of Fermanagh, was with him, and that the O'Hagans were not with him. So with his men, all tall men and valiant, Felim rode boldly to the crannog. It happened to be Friday, the 11th day of May, in the year of our Lord, 1593. The trees of the crannog were now green, and the orchard bright with apple blossom, white and red. Great smokes rolled from all the chimneys of the crannog. There were many tents, both on the island and on the shores of the lake. Felim sent word of his arrival to the Earl. The Earl would not see him that day, but he bade his people treat Felim with all the consideration due to his rank, for Felim was a great gentleman amongst the O'Neill nation. Accordingly they pitched a tent for him in the lawn, within the island, and Felim and his men lacked nothing of food, drink or attendance, but had good entertainment from the Earl. But neither on Saturday could Felim have access to the Earl, with whom there were divers great lords then in conference, for it was the eve of the great rebellion of the men of Ulster.

CHAPTER VII.

THE O'HAGANS COME TO CAMP.

THAT night, as it grew towards morning, Felim was awake in his tent and he heard the sound of hoofs of horses, and after that voices as of some commotion in the camp. There were three tents pitched on the lawn for Felim's people, close together for their greater security. Donnell Ogue, Heber, and Calvach slept with their dear lord Felim in the same tent. Felim awoke Heber, who slept at his head, and Heber arose and went forth out of the tent. It was already grey morning and the birds were twittering in the trees of the crannog.

Presently he returned and said :—" This is a bad arrival, dear master. The brethren of the slain man are here with a company of the Clan O'Hagan, and they are pitching their tents around the bridge-head." Felim and his men were not happy after that.

Next morning the Earl and the lord Maguire attended Mass at a very small church which was near the lake, and Felim went with them in their company, and the O'Hagans saluted him both in his going out and his coming in, and they said that as he had the Earl's pardon the feud was at an end. Felim after that felt more confidence, and forgot the words of his wife. In the afternoon the Earl and the lord Maguire rode together along the banks of the Bann. This was that lord who asked the Council to fix beforehand the eric of the sheriff whom they were sending into Fermanagh. After supper, in the evening, Felim stepped to the Earl and begged private conference, but the Earl would not confer with him that night. The next morning when the Earl gave audience in the great hall of the crannog, a pursuivant from the Castle of Dublin stepped before Felim and delivered a letter to the Earl. Whom when the Earl saw he broke out there stormfully before them all, saying in the Irish tongue, " By the Son of God I would rather be dead than looking at the like of you coming to me every day in your short red coats !" In those days the mind of the Earl was exceeding wrathful against the Lord Deputy on account of many wrongs and misdealings.

Though Felim afterwards had conference with the Earl, he did not prosper with his suit. After that the Earl and his beautiful young Countess, with one or two gentlemen went down to the Bann side and entered a boat. It was their purpose to row down the Bann and to dine at a place about five miles from the crannog.

Felim and his men accompanied the Earl to the river side and there went with him also the three O'Hagans—namely, Owen, and Henry, and Hugh Ogue. These brothers as they went conversed pleasantly with the whole company, and especially with Felim.

When the boat was leaving the shore, Felim standing hard by, cried aloud, " God be at one with thee till night, my lord !''

The Earl only answered, in a low voice, " God be at enmity with thee till the night !''

Felim did not hear this. His face was very pale, for his mind misgave him when he heard no reply from the Earl.

So the Earl and the Countess went down the river. Felim stood quite still looking after them from the shore.

Then the three brothers, Owen, Henry, and Hugh Ogue, came to him with flattering speeches.

Felim forgot the words of his wife on that occasion, for he was deceived by their flattering speeches and the gay and frank faces of the three brothers. He forgot all, even though Donnell Ogue, standing close to him, pulled him by the mantle secretly. So the whole party moved to the camp, with their backs to the bright Bann, and Owen O'Hagan went in front with Felim, by themselves, and as they went Owen put his left arm over Felim's shoulder and around his neck, and their joined shadows falling westward, were as one upon the green grass, for it was forenoon, and the sun still in his ascending.

The O'Hagans, as I have already mentioned, had pitched their tents beside the bridge head of the causeway which led over the lake to the crannog. Amongst the rest, hard by the gate of the bridge, they pitched one tent, spacious, of fine leather curiously stained, and they adorned it inside with great care. It was a tent for the slain youth. They arranged it for him as if he were there. They hung up their brother's hat and plume, and his helmet, and battle-dress and all his weapons of war.

His favourite hound was in that tent, and his two hawks sat there hooded upon their perch. Shane's war-horse too was tethered near it, and his horses for hunting ; and the tent was made ready in every respect as if their dear brother Shane were alive and well.

As Felim and Owen drew nigh to the camp the Clan O'Hagan stood at the doors of their tents.

Felim happened to say in the course of conversation—" I have not slept well of late."

Owen replied, " Thou wilt get over that ; thou wilt sleep well soon."

They were in front of the vacant tent when he said that. So saying he withdrew his arm from Felim's shoulder.

" Dost thou see a man in the door of this tent ?" he said.

" I see no man," said Felim.

" I do," said Owen. " I see a man there, in the prime of his youth and beauty, but his face is pale and bloody, and his yellow hair clotted with blood. (Have patience dear brother !) I think *thou* seest him too ; there, or somewhere ; O Felim ! son of Turlough, son of Art."

" Stand back from me !" cried Felim ; " there is death in thy looks."

" And in my heart, too," cried the other, and ere a man could see what was done there was a swift glittering, a flashing of steel in the bright sun and two blended screams—one of vengeance and one for help—and the glittering ceased, for the sword that glittered was through Felim.

Thereupon, Henry and Hugh Ogue ran up, and the three slew Felim there before their brother's tent and hewed him in pieces.

Felim's men ran from that slaughter. The rest fled along the bank of the river, but Donnell Ogue ran straight to the river pursued by the three brothers. He sprang into it and swam, but it was not his fortune that he should reach the further shore of the Bann, for Hugh Ogue snatched a long slender spear from one of the clansmen and poising, discharged it with all his force at Donnell Ogue as he swam and struck him between the shoulders. Donnell Ogue cried out with a loud voice, and sank in the bright waters of the Bann, drawing down the spear with him slowly till the waters covered it.

At the gate of the crannog, at the time when Owen turned upon Felim, there was a young man who was leading forth an ass. The ass had laden panniers on each side of him. The young man's name was Hugh O'Gallagher, the same whom the Earl had ordered to follow him with the provisions down the river. The young man stood still horror-stricken while the slaughter went forward, and it was a long time before he embarked. When he came to the place where the Earl and the Countess were, the Earl said : —

" What delayed thee ?"

Hugh O'Gallagher did not answer.

The Earl said again—" What delayed thee ?"

Hugh at last made answer—" Looking at a bad deed."

" What was that ?" said the Earl.

" The killing of Felim, son of Turlough,"
answered the other, " and he is killed, yea, and is
Donnell Ogue killed too—truly, both killed and
drowned."

When the Countess Mabel, the fair and young
daughter of the High Marshal of all Ireland, heard
that word, she cried out and beat both hands together, after the manner of women mourning for
the dead. To whom the Earl spake vehemently in
the English tongue, but inasmuch as he spake in
the English tongue it is not known what he said,
Then he turned to Hugh O'Gallagher and asked,
" What happened my shot (musketeers) that went
over the river?"

SIR RICHARD BINGHAM.

FROM time to time we either see the name of Bingham mentioned in the newspapers or meet persons of that name. It is not, indeed, a common name in Ireland, but also it is not an uncommon. There are Binghams in our peerage, there is a good deal of Bingham blood mingled in our western squirearchy, and Binghams are met with in every rank of life. Of the founder of this Anglo-Irish race I would supply the reader with a sketch as clear as I can make it within a limited space.

Sir Richard Bingham was in the year 1584, just four years before the Armada, appointed Governor of Connaught by Queen Elizabeth. He was already a distinguished soldier, but little anticipated the sort of warfare which awaited him in Connaught, or dreamt that under that pressure the latent ferocity of his character would so come out as to render it a doubtful question whether he was a great warrior and administrator, or a great historical ruffian. Sir Richard did not cross the Shannon alone. He was a clannish man, and brought with him quite a brigade of Binghams. He was a younger son, with many brothers and cousins. There came with him John Bingham and Jacob

Bingham, and George the Greater and George the Less, and divers others of the name. In fact, the Western Irish gentry regarded him as the chief of a new sept, and generally wrote of him as chief of his tribe.

At this time the people of Connaught were judged and governed by their chieftains. Sir Richard governed the chieftains, but the chieftains like mediæval nobles, governed the people. About this time Sir John Perrott induced the chieftains to surrender their power and voluntarily to extinguish themselves as petty kings. This they did under a celebrated instrument of State called the " Composition of Connaught." Whoever visits the Record Office in the Four Courts, will see that Composition deed with the signatures or marks of all the western chiefs duly appended. Under this instrument every chief surrendered his power and his lands, which under tanistry he only held for life. In return he got a fixed proportion of the tribe lands in *tail male,* his principal vassals got their share fixed too, with " judicial " rents payable to the chief. With these rents and his fixed proportion of the tribal lands the deposed chief had to content himself. Thereafter he could not go about coshering amongst his vassals, " cutting and spending," exacting coigne and livery, etc. These doltish old customs," as Sir Richard called them, were abolished. In fact, it was a sort of agrarian revolution not unlike that which has been witnessed in our own times, with this difference, that it was then the gentry—the landlords so to speak—who benefited by the change. For example, all the considerable gentlemen of the county of Mayo were then relieved from the unlimited exactions of the Lord Burke, head of the Burkes of Mayo. No change was made in the position of the peasantry, but the gentry were made free of the chieftains. They got their estates in *tail,* and judicial fixed rents ; they were rooted in the soil, and Sir Richard and the State looked to them to maintain the new order as a great conservative element, much in the same way as some of our statesmen to-day look with similar hopes to our new peasant proprietors.

It was, I say, a great social and agrarian revolution, and Sir Richard won great *kudos* for the manner in which it was carried out. Nor were his hopes frustrated. The new proprietors to the utmost of their ability sustained Sir Richard. In all his wars and in all his devastations and outrages, Sir Richard had the bulk of the western gentry on his side. Speaking generally, he had Connaught at his back in all his doings, good and also bad. We read of high gentlemen lifting up their voices and weeping aloud when* they learned that they were at last free from the government of the great chieftains.

* See, for example, *Calendar of State Papers, Ireland,* September 27th, 1589.

Those great chieftains were indeed a wonderful race of men ; but if they were swifter than eagles and stronger than lions, one must remember that lions and eagles are bound to have many foes.

Well, the ink was hardly dry upon " Composition of Connaught," and on that of Thomond or Clare, which settled separately, when the chieftains began to repent—began to sigh for the old free quarters, for their cosherings and free suppers, their armed retinues and the gallows which stood beside their hall-doors, the symbol of their power and pride. One of the Southern chieftains rebelled. Sir Richard, with Connaught behind him, went down to visit the recalcitrant, slew him, hanged the garrison, broke down " the west wall of his castle," Clanowen Castle, " from top to bottom," and returned victorious. " That exploit," say the chroniclers, " exalted the fame and honour of Sir Richard, for there was not on dry land a stronger castle than that." But now the great lords in the north of the province too began to kick against the Composition. Sir Richard marched against them and, still sustained by public opinion and the forces of the Province, " plagued " the insurgent lords terribly. The word is a favourite one in his despatches, derived from *plaga,* a stroke. The reader now must picture to himself some fifteen years of the most desperate and horrible warfare in which Sir Richard Bingham, exhibiting a preternatural activity and the highest fighting qualities, and backed always by the bulk of the province, almost ceaselessly battered upon the great lords, asserting against them the Composition of Connaught. As the horrible strife went on—for on their side too the chieftains exhibited a determination as great as his own—the innate ferocity of the man came more and more to the surface. On one occasion he hanged three little children of the best blood in Connaught as forfeited pledges, though the Chief Justice of Connaught warned him that the hanging was illegal. He hanged O'Conor Roe, "who was nearly 100 years old"—I quote here from the State papers. One of his captains, out on a raid, called to a woman with a child in her arms, "come kiss me, darling," or words to that effect. When she drew nigh, trembling, he ran his sword through the infant and the young mother's breast. His name was John Gilson. The Government ordered Gilson to prison. Bingham defied the Government, released him, and put him on the Council of Connaught. By the way, this Gilson was an Irishman—in fact nearly all Bingham's people were Irish. At one place Bingham's men were slaughtering women and children. Some women took to the sea and tried to swim away ; his soldiers killed them with stones. There was no punishment. But on the other hand, if Bingham was a tiger he was also a lion—such a warrior and such an administrator, so far as his power extended, Connaught never saw before or since. He had no fear either of God or man, and would drive the Composition over Connaught though he had to invoke the aid of the devil in doing so.

The reader must form his own conception of this strange being. He left no posterity. The noble families of that name descend from his brothers and cousins. There alone in the 16th century driving forward the Composition of Connaught stands this terrible figure begrimed with powder smoke and stained with blood, innocent as well as guilty. But the West of Ireland went with Bingham in all that work, and that is a strange and significant fact. Bingham led the majority in a civil war. Bingham in one of his letters written when his career was about closing says : — " I scarce ever had any aid save from the Irishry of my province." Once the Government sent him 200 English soldiers ; Bingham disarmed them and gave their weapons to his Connaughtmen.

THE OUTLAWED CHIEFTAIN.

INTRODUCTION.

ONE of the most romantic incidents in the history of Elizabethan Ireland is the well-known story of the capture and captivity in Dublin and the escape thence of the famous warrior Hugh Roe O'Donnell. The flight was effected on Christmas Eve, 1591. After adventures and sufferings which I have elsewhere described, he was borne half dead with cold and hunger across the Wicklow hills, then covered with deep snow, into the wild gorge of Glenmalure to the protection of a warlike chieftain, Feagh MacHugh O'Byrne, whose principal stronghold was in that romantic glen. The boy's feet were frost-bitten and lamed. He was straightway put to bed, to use the phraseology of the times, "laid upon a bed of healing," and carefully nursed and tended by the old chieftain's best leeches. So Christmas time passed for the much-wronged Hugh Roe. Through the windows of his little hut he saw the snow-clad mountains, caught the gleam of a passing morion or polished battleaxe head as the chieftain's trusty sentinels paced to and fro. He heard the curious sounds incident to the daily life of Feagh's semi-barbarous mediæval stronghold, and the murmurings of Avonbeg swollen with melting snow rushing forward and downward to join the Avonmore. As he grew stronger faces famous in Irish history came and went about his couch, faces very kind and friendly to him, though terrible enough to the then rulers of Ireland. There came old Feagh the warrior and spoiler, and his wife the Lady Rose O'Byrne, the last reference to whom that I have discovered is an Order in Council that she should be burnt in the Castle Yard, presumably for high treason. There came Feagh's sons, Turlough and Felim and Raymond, all characters of historical dignity and interest ; his son-in-law, the Brown Geraldine ; and, not to extend the list of Hugh Roe's kind Glenmalure friends, Feagh's foster-son, Anthony O'More, chieftain designate, as I may say, of the Queen's County, which from time immemorial had been O'More territory, though now mainly occupied by grantees and Crown tenants. His name Anthony was shortened and softened into Owny ; as Owny he figures in all contemporary documents, English and Irish. He was eldest son of a celebrated warrior and chieftain of the Queen's County named Rory Ogue O'More, and was at this time about the same age as Hugh Roe, that is to say, about nineteen. As every one was then known by a patronymic title, the boy's full style was Owny mac Rory Ogue O'More. A short time before this the Viceroy Fitzwilliam, whose eyes were fixed upon the lad wrote concerning him to Burleigh : — " Owny mac Rory Ogue O'More hath lately taken weapon " (i.e., been solemnly invested with arms and knighted.) " He is a lad of a bold and stirring spirit. The O'Mores look to him to be their captain." This boy became very famous afterwards in the Tyrone wars. There is a likeness of him in the first plate of the *Pacata Hibernia,* which has been reproduced in Miss Lawless's History of Ireland, in " The Story of the Nations " series. This fine boy, as yet without a stain of blood on his hands, was one of Hugh Roe's kind friends and frequent visitors when he lay on his couch of healing at Glenmalure. His father, Rory Ogue, is the chief character in the story which I am about to relate.

A few miles from Glenmalure, at Newcastle, there was settled these years an English gentleman of high birth and considerable influence in the State. He was Sir Harry Harrington, nephew of Sir Henry Sidney, and therefore first cousin of Sir Philip. Sir Harry Harrington of Newcastle and old Feagh of Glenmalure were good friends and neighbours. They were quite intimate and neighbourly —a curious and significant fact, for Sir Harry was a member of the Council, and Feagh was in fact anything but a pillar of the State. Whoever observed Sir Harry closely would have seen that he lacked the little finger of the right hand, and whoever saw him stripped saw a body cut and scarred like a carbonado. Who did all this cutting and carving upon the body of Sir Harry Harrington of Newcastle? It was Rory Ogue O'More, father of Owny, Hugh Roe's new friend, and it is the story of that cutting and carving which I am about to relate. Rory Ogue and Sir Harry are the chief actors in the story, the incidents of which I have collected from the Sidney State Papers, the Calendar of State Papers (Ireland), the notes of Sir John Harrington's translation of Ariosto, the Four Masters, Derrick's "Image of Ireland," and Philip O'Sullivan's *Historia Hiberniæ*. In telling the story I assume the classical privilege of occasionally putting speeches into the mouths of the chief characters—speeches such as under the circumstances they were likely to have delivered.

CHAPTER I.

RORY OGUE O'MORE.

IN the year 1575 Sir Henry Sidney, "Big Henry of the Beer," as the Four Masters affectionately style him, came for the last time into Ireland as Chief Governor of the realm. Along with him came his nephew, Harry Harrington, the history of whose severe woundings and bodily harms I desire to tell.

Young Harrington was by Sir Henry appointed to the most dangerous and stirring service at the time to be found in Ireland—viz., that of the Queen's County, the ancient kingdom or principality of Leix. There the nation of the O'Mores were in fierce rebellion under their captain, Rory Ogue O'More, and young Harrington was bound to see there a great deal of warlike work of a peculiar and Irish variety. The land question in Leix was in course of solution according to 16th century methods. It was, indeed, a most burning question, literally so ; it had reduced to cinders not only Leix but a considerable proportionate of the adjoining counties of Carlow, Meath, Dublin, Offaly, Kildare and Kilkneny. Rory Ogue, in assertion of alleged ancestral rights there, which were denied by the Government, had wasted and burnt far and wide, burnt the open country and a great many walled towns, till the name of Rory was a terror in the land, and women silenced crying children with Rory's dreadful name. Rory turns up throughout the State Papers in as many forms as that old sea-god with whom Ulysses grappled in the midst of his seals. Now he was an army with banners and bag-pipes, cavalry and infantry, now a swift troop of plunderers destroying and fleeing, fleeing and destroying ; his course, traceable in the night by lines of burning houses, in the day by pillars of smoke and the wailing of women. We find him a buttress of the State leaning on and leant on by the Government. We find him the turbulent lord besieging the castles of his neighbours, annexing the lands of his neighbours, while the weak Government, affecting slumber, looked out as it were with one eye half unclosed, on the let alone principle. For our chieftainry, like the English baronage, asserted the right of private war, and the Government acquiesced. Thus, we find in the annals for this reign, the following curious entry—" Ulick, son of Richard Sassenagh, Earl of Clanricarde, and his brother Shane of the Clover, were at war with each other this year, but they were both at peace with the Government." Anon, Rory, sheathing his sword, rides to Dublin, to Court, as a great lord with his lifeguard and feudal retinue, creating a flutter in viceregal circles as well by his lofty bearing and his size, for he was a giant in stature, as by the fame of his exploits. Anon, he is on the warpath again, and this time against the State. Sometimes Rory was not heard of for weeks or months. Men hoped that he was dead or fled. The wasted lands revived, burnt towns and villages were timidly rebuilt, flocks and herds began to graze again in Leix. Here and there a timorous husbandman drove a scant furrow, praying God and his saints to keep Rory Ogue away. Men spoke of Rory as a thing of the past, and recounted dreadful tales as of ancient days. Suddenly, without

premonitory symptoms, the chieftain again, in all
his terrors and horrors, burst upon the half-settled
country. He had been under leeches on " a bed of
healing," had been in the south secretly with the
Graces and Butlers, or on the other side of the
Shannon with Shane of the Clover, a congenial
spirit, refitting his shattered fortunes, collecting
means for the renewal of the truceless war. Sometimes he was a prince, sometimes a Robin Hood.
Now he was the hospitable feudal lord, dispensing
a flowing hospitality to English and Irish alike, and
anon the terror of the land, slaughtering and burning
English and Irish without distinction ; or a fugitive
and an outlaw drinking water out of his shoe, and
with a long stick toasting steaks cut from the loins
of a stolen ox. Yet, the wife of this thief was first
cousin to the Earl of Ormond, who, with the Earls
of Leicester and Essex, kept the barriers in jousts
before the Queen. Rory Ogue was in fact one of the
first gentlemen of Ireland. Such was life then. Nor
was there anything very peculiar in his career ; it was
Irish and Elizabethan and quite according to custom.
Given a certain combination of circumstances, let
Court breezes sit but for a while in a certain quarter,
and the Earl of Ormond himself, playfellow of
Edward VI, patron of Spenser, one of the greatest
nobles of the Empire, would lead just such a life ;
to-day a pillar of the State, to-morrow a plunderer,
passing through the land like a plague, his eye not

sparing children ; anon, a fugitive stealing one cow, and on a long stick broiling steaks cut from her side, just like Rory. A great western chief once led such a life, yet he married the widow of Sir Philip Sidney, who was also widow of Robert, Earl of Essex. Rory must not be all mistaken for a rapparee. He was, as I have said, one of the great gentlemen of the realm. Great lords filed petitions of right against the Crown so, and not un-frequently, by sticking manfully to their work, carried off all the honours and profits of the con-troversy. Rory Ogue's western ally, Shane of the Clover, and Shane's brother, Ulick, Earl of Clanricarde, wrung their own terms from the Government by downright war and rebellion ; and the Earl of Ormond, too, in a manner and by deputy, played the same high game and won.

Who had the right in this controversy of Rory Ogue O'More *versus* the Queen ? Frankly, I cannot tell. It would require a volume adequately to set out the mere facts of the controversy, and the arguings *pro* and *con* would fill another. Rory at least, was perfectly certain that he was in the right. It was not for a claim in which he only half believed that the O'More, lord of many castles and rent-producing lands, converted himself into a demon of the pit, breathing flame and suffering himself as much pain as he inflicted. But he was O'More, had rights inherited from afar, nigh 2,000 years old. These he would uphold against all men, and rather be rolled into his grave than surrender.

There is really something almost sublime in the manner in which these Elizabethan lords grappled with injurious governments, in the desperate resolution with which they on their side stripped for the duel, ready to endure all things and inflict all things. Such a stript chieftain, his own land first wasted and his own castles first broken, almost audibly addressed the ruling powers thus : — "Here, O injurious Viceroy, I stand and defy you. Death has no terrors for me, nor has cold or famine, nor the slaughter of my people, nor wakeful nights and laborious days. I defy you, Lord Deputy, and Hell at your back ; and put me to the proof now, and you will find Hell going out of me."

We have seen landlords in our time rolled out of their estates much more ignobly. But these rebel lords of the Elizabethan age were a tough and stubborn breed. I sometimes feel as if such men as Rory Ogue had gathered into themselves the very strength of the elements, according to that strange Pagan incantation which figures as one verse in St. Patrick's hymn : —

> " I bind to myself to-day
> The swiftness of the wind,
> The power of the sea,
> The hardness of rocks,
> The endurance of the earth," etc., etc.

CHAPTER II.

SIR HENRY SIDNEY ON THE SITUATION

SUCH was the enemy with whom young Harry Harrington was called upon by his uncle to contend. "It is the gap of danger, dear Harry,"—Sir Henry said as he gave the lad his last instructions—"the gap of danger and a forlorn hope. Our sweet Saviour shield thee, my dear nephew, from the bullets and battle-axes of that blood-stained villain. Leix is the unbarred door of the fortress and the ingate of the Pale. If Rory drives us thence, all our many enemies in those regions have a free inroad into the heart of the settled country. The O'Conors of Offaly, the O'Carrolls of Ely, the Foxes, M'Geoghegans, and Tyrrells of Westmeath, will confederate themselves under him as captain, and the O'Byrnes and O'Tooles on this side, joining hands with him, will raise again the discontented Geraldines of Kildare, for the Earl is not too well affected to the State, and he is led at will by his kinsmen. If Rory wins, the traitor Ormond will be at his old work again, playing Royalist at Court, while his savage brethren and all his nation prey and burn the loyal subject. Don't trust a Butler, Harry, not the length of the lane. If Rory wins, Ormond wins, and the House of Sydney is disgraced and overthrown. But he will not win. I have sworn never again to make peace with him save on my own terms. He came to me in Kilkenny, and knelt before me in the Cathedral Church. He had a full advantage of my then distress and perplexities, harassed as I was by Ormond and his brute ally the Ox.* Such slaugh-- terings and burnings as Rory's I thought that I never should forgive, but I was enforced, and now he is out again, and has overthrown the shire, and makes prey on the good subject over all the Midlands. There are a thousand pounds on his head by proclamation. That ought to serve well. Trust not the Englishmen over much. Even here, around Dublin, I know too well the false hearts of the Palesmen, and the new comers are hardly a whit more reliable. Don't trust them over much, for by marriage or by interest and secret treaties, they are often closely allied with the rebels. Neither too much distrust the Irish. Amongst the worst of those rebel natives the Queen has staunch friends. No man in Ireland has been friendlier to myself, or more serviceable to the State, than Turlough Lynagh, The O'Neill, or a deadlier enemy to myself and to the State than Ormond. At the worst, dear Harry, warring in Leix and on Rory Ogue thou wilt learn what Irish

* A private nickname of Sidney's for the Earl of Thomond.

war is like. An thou canst capture or kill that fierce villain Rory, or induce or compel him to accept decent terms, thy reputation is secured. For myself, why, Sidney will then unbuckle his harness with right goodwill and lay down his offices. Then for my gardens and my books, and a peaceful mug of homebrewed ale. Try this, Harry, good ' Saxon ale of bitterness,' lad, not the sweet stuff that these islanders delight in. My Irish friends, as thou knowest, have pleasantly nicknamed me Henri Mor na Beora, that is to say, ' Big Henry of the Beer.' Well they may ; I love the liquor, and have made it serve me too. With beer I conquered the Butlers, and clipped the wings of high-flying Black Tom. Drink from the *mether*. Nay, lad, the corner, the corner ! I shan't put on my sister's son, and a boy, the jest I played on some fine gentlemen at court. Be governed by circumstances, Harry, as they arise. Thy associate in the government will be one who assuredly ought to understand his business, Alexander Cosby, son of Francis. If the lad is a tithe as good as the father he will do well, though I profess such butcherly soldiers art not much to my liking," etc., etc.

Sidney (Big Harry of the Beer), though not free from the criminality which characterised statesmen of that wicked age was, on the whole, a highminded, generous and loyal sort of man, handsome, of a fine presence, huge and bulky in stature, merry and witty, and extremely courteous, a worthy father of that paragon of chivalry, Sir Philip. The story of how he conquered the Butlers with beer is amusing. When he invaded Tipperary, the Butlers' country, his army fell into a panic. They felt like boys entering a den full of "unpastured dragons." Sidney gathered them together, speeched them, and set a great many barrels of beer flowing. Under the mingled effect of oratory and strong ale the army plucked up its heart. The soldiers declared they would kill him if he did not lead them against the Butlers, and that night nothing was heard in camp but the singing of war-songs, whistling of war-tunes, sharpening of swords, and imprecations on the whole breed, seed, and generation of the Butlers.

CHAPTER III.

YOUNG HARRY HARRINGTON GOES NORTH TO WAR.

So young Harrington, with troops provided by his uncle, full of young confidence and vainglory, went down to that burned and blasted country, associated himself with Alexander Cosby, and marched to and fro defending the country against Rory, who was at the time unable to make head against his enemies in the open field. For a while the Viceroy received good tidings. One day, however, came a pale messenger out of Leix and stood before Sir Henry. Such a face pulled Priam's curtains. "Your Honour, I bring bad news from Leix. Alexander Cosby and Harry Harrington are prisoners with Rory Ogue. He took them at a parley, and where they are now no one knows."

Here was an untoward revolution of fortune's wheel. Rory Ogue had now a hostage worth the pecuniary value of the whole of the blasted and burned territory, and was determined to utilise his advantage to the uttermost. On the heels of that doleful messenger came another, Rory's ambassador or pursuivant, stating the terms on which the outlawed chief would submit to the Government. But Sir Henry, though ready to pay every penny he could spare to save the life of his sister's son, would not as the Queen's Deputy consent to Rory's high territorial demands. He felt that concession here would be a blow to his honour and a serious injury to the prestige of the State. Rory permitted him to open communications with the prisoner, and young Harrington wrote to the Viceroy saying, " I will die rather than give my consent to those conditions. Never mind my worthless life."

I have always thought that Ireland is the richer

for every brave and generous act performed by any one upon her soil, whether stranger or native. Sir Henry's loyalty to the State on this occasion and his nephew's submission to his fate, are quite in the early Roman style. Those noble historians, the Irish Four Masters would have been quick enough to recognise, and that generously, the behaviour of these brave Englishmen.

In short, though Rory had his hostages he could make nothing out of them. Harrington was ready to die, and Sir Henry willing that he should die rather than see The O'More triumph at the expense of the State. Rory hesitated and pondered, and while he pondered the wheel of fortune took another turn disastrous to Rory. Rory keeping a firm grip on his valuable pair of hostages, lay low for the time. He had dismissed the bulk of his forces with orders to hold themselves in readiness at call. Of these hostages, the second, Alexander Cosby, was son to one of the remarkable men of the age. When the Queen's County was confiscated and made shire land by Philip and Mary, Francis Cosby, one of the bravest, and also one of the cruellest and most ferocious men of his time, was appointed captain of the shire. Whether a hero or a ruffian, or, as is most probable, a mixture of both, he was certainly not a man to be despised, and fought his hot corner as well as any hot corner was ever fought before or since. Concerning him I excerpt the following anecdote from the pages of an old historian. From my knowledge of the condition of society prevailing then in Leix I have little doubt that the story is substantially true.

"Francis Cosby usually resided at Stradbally. Before his hall-door there grew a tree of great size with many wide-extending boughs. Upon this tree he used to hang not only men but women, and also male children. When women hanging from ropes dangled out of the tree, and when their babes hung beside them, throttled in tresses of their mother's hair, he used to experience an incredible satisfaction. On the other hand, when the tree had no suspended bodies, he used to address it in this wise : ' O, my tree, you seem to be affected by a great sorrow. No wonder, you are so long bare. But O tree I shall soon abate your grief ; soon with bodies I shall adorn your boughs.' "

But there were barbarous reprisals upon Cosby's people too ; of that we may be sure.

Attended by the most valiant and faithful of his men—Rory retired with Harrington and Cosby into the most secret of his fastnesses. It was in the depth of a forest somewhere on the borders of the county of Carlow. I don't find anywhere in Elizabethan Ireland that thorough loyalty of the clan to the chief which Sir Walter Scott so celebrates in his pictures of Highland society. In all the Irish clans there was a party in secret or open opposition to the elected chief, and the Queen had allies in every territory into which she sent her captains. On the other hand, the faithfulness of the chieftain's personal retinue, of the men who lived at his board and had the charge of his person, was above reproach. Their honour was inviolate, and forms one of the most beautiful features of that strange period. Here in his forestine retreat The O'More kept watch over his hostages pending the issue. Along with him was his brother, a priest. Rory was a devout man in his own way. In feudal hall or under the greenwood tree this faithful brother said Mass for Rory and shrived him. There was also with Rory a certain Cormac O'Connor, a gentleman who had been educated at the Court of England, but who, his claims on the adjoining King's County having been denied by the Government, had joined his fortunes with those of The O'More. Another unexpected sharer of the plunderer's wild existence was his wife. Rory, by way of clearing the decks for action, had first disposed of his children. They were entrusted to the secret keeping of friends beyond the limits of the war-theatre. A famous De Burgo chief at the other side of the Shannon, sheltered some of them. But Rory's faithful wife would not leave him. The Lady Margaret would taste the bitter with her lord as she had tasted the sweet. When Rory " went out " his wife went out with him, rode by him in his campaign and forays, cowered low with him in the woods and mountains when his star was obscured. Elizabethan Ireland supplies many women of this heroic type.

CHAPTER IV.

RORY CHASTISES HIS TRAPPER WITH RESULTS.

Now in Rory's household there was a traitor. This person was by profession a trapper and in position, I suppose, a sort of slave. When plundered beef was not forthcoming he helped to stock the chieftain's larder with hares, rabbits, and an occasional deer. Amongst these proud men of war and gentlemen, he was a lonely and melancholy wight, a butt when they were merry, a thing to breathe themselves upon when enraged. He shared all the danger and none of the reward or the glory. Any day the branch of a Queen's County tree might bear his pendent body. Curious servile thoughts, much dumb discontent passed through his gloomy spirit as he sat watching his gins and toils waiting for the cry which told that some poor creature of the forest had come to grief. The glitter of gold, too, came and went in the dark places of his mind.

There was a sum of £1,000 on the head of the man who ate his rabbits and perhaps never said " Thank you, *venator.*" Rory thought as little of the trapper as of his foot-leather—serviceable stuff, his own. No one gave the sorry wight a thought or deemed that any danger could arise from such a slave. One day the trapper offended the chieftain ; he was seen conversing with suspicious persons, or had been idle in his venatorial office or insolent to his superiors, or had committed some other breach of law or etiquette in the little company gathered there under the greenwood tree. The chief prescribed a flogging for the trapper, and thought no more of the matter. With aching sides and shoulders the servile man returned to his gins and toils, but there was a dangerous fire kindled in his breast. His name we don't know. Whenever our historians meet with a plebeian they withhold the name. Why should such fellows have a name at all ? Nevertheless even in feudal Ireland they helped to make history.

CHAPTER V.

CAPTAIN HARPOL AND THE TRAPPER.

CAPTAIN HARPOL, commanding a detachment of the Royal army, lay in garrison in the Castle of

Carlow, his thoughts much occupied with Rory Ogue. Indeed, it was hard for him to forget Rory, for Rory's mark was distinguishable wherever the Captain's eyes might turn. All around the castle were blackened ruins of houses, for Carlow, in spite of its castle and its strong walls, had been sacked and burnt by the terrible omnipresent Rory. Black gaunt ruins showed dolefully through the trees over the plains, the remains of country gentlemen's seats, of farmsteads and huts, destroyed by the same hand. Rory had left a dreadful mark upon five or six Irish counties. All the land around Carlow was waste and empty. The curse of Rory lay heavy along the shores of the Barrow. The peasantry had fled. Even Harpol's cattle fed only under the eye of Harpol's soldiers. Armed men watched them as they grazed, and at night drove them within the bawn of the castle, and locked and barred the gates. No one knew when or where Rory might next break out. From the Shannon to the Liffey all the midlands were a theatre for the vengeance of O'More. The fear of the great spoiler was over all the land.

Rory may have been thinking of Harpol this day, for, indeed, he was not far distant. Harpol most assuredly was thinking of Rory, and not pleasantly. Robert Harpol had an estate in Leix long since reduced to ashes and wilderness by the enraged chieftain; the charred ruins of Carlow lay under

his eyes, perhaps the smoke of them in his nostrils.
Yet Robert Harpol was a stout and brave man, as,
indeed, were most of the Queen's captains at this
time. If the chieftains were brave, the captains were
equally brave. A soldier interrupted the meditations
of Captain Harpol. "Your honour, there is a
countryman below who hath tidings for your private
ear—of great moment—of Rory Ogue."

In a moment the Constable was all alive.

"Yes, I will see him."

Enter now a rustical, shock-headed wight, indeed
a very salvage man, with bright, small eyes peering
through his matted glibb, and carrying nets upon
his arm—in short, our friend the trapper, his loins
and back still sore from Rory's punitory thong.
The trapper's countenance, I fancy, was not comely
at the best, nor could it have been improved by the
passions which drove him thither—viz., revenge
and love of gold. Yet to Harpol it was a face
full of interest. Having louted low and glanced
around him suspiciously, the salvage man drew nigh
to the Captain, and unloaded himself of his secret,
confidentially and familiarly, but in a fierce whisper,
"Rory Ogue, with only thirty swords, is in the
forest of ——, Harrington and Cosby with him. I
know the place, your honour, and will bring you
there and the sodgers—for a trifle." The delighted
Constable did not haggle with the fellow about
terms.

CHAPTER VI.

CAPTAIN HARPOL'S MIDNIGHT SWOOP.

As the shades of evening fell two hundred soldiers ranked themselves in the castle yard, silently without bugle call or other noise of preparation. Glad was the stout captain. This night's work, if successful, would bring to him great renown and also £1,000 in gold *minus* the trapper's stipulated fee : and remember, £1,000 then was worth possibly £15,000 now.

The night was wild and wet. No moon or star lit Harpol upon his way, only the experienced mind of the trapper, who, guarded by soldiers for fear of treachery, plodded heavily forward in front of the column with his nets on his arm. With these he would not part. In his servile mind he had a purpose which will presently be disclosed. Through the moaning forest, under the tossing boughs, over soft and hard, in the teeming darkness all followed the trapper. At last he paused. The soldiers stood still, and Harpol stepped up to the guide. It was Rory's camp or fastness and consisted of a single good-sized house thatched with sods and bracken or rushes. It showed dimly through the night. All was wrapped in silence and slumber, the inmates dreaming such dreams as visit outlaws and plunderers.

CHAPTER VII.

THE TRAPPER'S HIGH OPINION OF THE VALUE OF TRAPS.

" This is the place," whispered the trapper. " See the house, Captain. Well, there he is. Rory is there, himself and his wife, and Cormac O'Conor, and the priest ; and there in handlocks he has Harrington and Cosby. But whisper again," murmured the glibbed one. Harpol inclined helmet and martial ear. " Captain, you'll never kill him or take him less than I help you. Sure we all know Rory Ogue. He'll bang ye all hither and over and around the door with his sword, and then he'll run this way down the bohareen into the wood. Captain, do you see this net ?" It was dark, but probably the Captain did notice the tenacity with which the fellow stuck to his toils. " Well, Captain, I'll just spread the net here between the trees in the bohareen, and by the hand of O'More, but I'll hould him nately the same as I would a shtag." Even in the excitement of the moment Harpol and his friends could not forbear laughing : under their breaths surely, at the trapper's undisguised poor opinion of their prowess, and his confidence in his own art of venery or the chase. Bidding the trapper, in some unrecorded Elizabethan phrase, " go to the deuce for a fool," Harpol prepared for the attack.

CHAPTER VIII.

RORY OGUE EXHIBITS TERRIBLE SWORD PLAY.

FROM the house two ways led into the forest. Both these Harpol beset, and with the rest of his men approached the house, marched up to the door, and bade his men break in. At the noise of the axes crashing through the door Rory awoke—all awoke. What an awakening ! Seizing his sword, Rory sprang first at his captives where they lay, Harry Harrington and Alexander Cosby, and slashed at them four or five times in the dark. Calling loudly to his men, and bidding his wife and brother keep close behind him, Rory opened the door, and stepped out in the midst of his enemies, making terrible sword play as he went. The bright steel flashed this way and that, showering sparks into the night from the stricken armour of those who barred his path. The very sound of his voice, shouting the O'More war-cry, had terror in it. Men believed that Rory Ogue was superhuman, and even Sir John Harrington, the accomplished courtier and author, tells us he was an enchanter and wrought spells. Moreover, he was of great stature, and his slashings and cuttings must have been hard to endure. Stout Captain Harpol came to the aid of his men the more readily inasmuch as Rory was in his shirt, and he himself in complete steel, but soon reeled back from a tremendous blow which stunned, but did not kill him, for it alit upon his helmet. Slashing to right and left, —one wishes that the trapper had got a slash—Rory broke through the ranks of armed men, ran down the lane, and escaped into the forest. Had Harpol but taken the servile man's advice, and allowed him to spread his net in that bohareen, he would have netted not only the great spoiler, but £1,000 of good money, *minus* the trapper's fee, that night.

"Rory Ogue crept between our legs like a serpent," said Harpol's men afterwards in explanation of their poltroonery. "He sprang over our heads like a deer." "He practised magic against us and made our weapons softer than butter." What is certain is that The O'More through his strength and valour and sudden upbursting of Celtic battle-fury broke through Captain Harpol's company of well-armed men. Around Rory the ranks opened or were burst asunder by his sword-play, but closed again like stormy waters behind him. His heroic wife, the Lady Margaret O'More, was slain at his heels. So was his faithful brother. All the

rest seeking to follow in the wake of the terrible
Rory, were slain or driven back into the house.
Harpol's men poured in pell-mell after them, and
within there in the darkness a murder grim and great
was committed, Harpol's men even killing each
other in the wild melee.

When the awful work was over and ignited
torches shed a ghastly light upon the scene, the
two prisoners were disengaged from the dead bodies.
Alexander Cosby did not show a scratch; poor
Harrington was a bleeding mass of cuts and
wounds. Four or five of these were the work of
Rory, the rest were given by Rory's men, and by
Harpol's in the fierce *mêlée* in the dark. How
happened it that Alexander Cosby had no wound,
while young Harrington had fourteen ? " An accident," said Cosby, " as I am a gentleman, a sheer
accident." Nevertheless it turned out to be a bad
accident for Cosby. Soon some ill-natured person
suggested that he had sheltered himself under
young Harrington's body, using it as a shield,
which he could easily do if the first blow or two had
made Harrington insensible. Whether this story
was seriously believed or not, it ran round the island
as a good military jest if nothing else, and
Alexander Cosby never got the better of it. We
can see him drop out of the saga without regret.
The only other fact I remember about Alexander
Cosby is that he had a wife named Dorcas.

Poor Harrington was conveyed away desperately wounded.   He had fourteen wounds in all, as counted by his cousin, Sir John Harrington.   His head was laid open.   Sir Henry Sidney tells us that he could see his nephew's brain move.   But all the fourteen wounds were found medicable save one.   He lost for ever the little finger of his right hand.

Harrington lived for many years afterwards in the castle called New Castle, County Wicklow. Dublin cyclers are perpetually riding past the ruins of his castle, and past the little broken church hard by where he worshipped.   Sir Philip Sidney was once here too, and prayed in the same little church. Our cyclers as they flit past might, with advantage, remember these things.   Sir Harry Harrington was appointed Captain of Wicklow, and exercised a sort of command there over the O'Byrnes and O'Tooles.   He and old Feagh MacHugh became good friends, but kept their friendship a secret.

CHAPTER IX.

CONCLUSION.

In Sir Henry's household was a gentleman of a literary turn of mind called Derrick.   He wrote a a book, of which Sir Henry is the hero and Rory

Ogue the villain, and adorned it with numerous plates, in most of which Rory Ogue is the central figure. It is called " The Image of Ireland," and is a very curious and interesting monument of the times.

It was imagined that Rory could never lift up his head again after this business. Derrick was delighted. He had a plate made for his " Image of Ireland," in which the great Rory, " whose thoughts did match the rolling sky," is represented utterly alone wandering through the forest. Behind him wolves are prowling around, expecting soon to sate their hunger on the flesh of the great spoiler. The book contains one long poem which is put into Rory's mouth, while in this woful situation, " uttering the same most lamentably with brynishe salte tears, wolfishe tears." It begins :—
      " I Rori Ogge inhabitant of Leiske "
and is not such doggrel as one might expect. Such is Derrick's Rory Ogue. But such was not by any means the Rory of history. Even after this blow we find him in the field once more, with hundreds of warriors, foot and horse, and fighting pitched battles with his Irish and English enemies.

He was eventually slain in battle by the Chief of the MacGilla-Patricks or Fitz-Patricks, June 30, 1578. Sir Henry Sidney was not a little proud of this feat, which was performed under his auspices.

Rory's death is thus commemorated in the Annals

—" Rory Ogue, son of Rory, son of Conall O'More, fell by the hand of Brian Ogue, son of Brian MacGilla-Patrick, and that Rory was the chief spoiler and insurgent of the men of Ireland in his time, and no one was disposed to fire a shot against the Crown for a long time after that."

Rory's sons were scattered abroad over Ireland under the care of friendly lords and chieftains. Feagh MacHugh brought up the bravest of them, Owney. For years Feagh held this brave youth like a war-hound in the slips. Three years after Hugh Roe visited Glenmalure, Feagh slipped him, and like a hound, gallant Owney flew straight upon his quarry. In short Rory's son conquered back the Queen's County, and held it for many years with a strong hand, and became more powerful and famous even than his father.

BRIAN OF-THE-RAMPARTS
O'ROURKE.

In Bingham's time the strongest chief in the West
of Ireland was The O'Rourke, Brian na Murtha,
Lord of Leitrim. This chieftain was a tall and
remarkably handsome man. His most distinguishing
characteristic was pride. All the Lord Deputies and
Presidents who had anything to do with him remarked upon this trait. " He was the proudest
man with whom I had to do in my time," wrote Sir
Henry Sidney. " The proudest man who walks
upon the earth to-day," wrote Malby. " The
proud beggar—the insolent, drunken proud
beggar !" wrote the fiercer and more abusive
Bingham. As to the charge of drunkenness, I can
only say this : I have myself seen in the Record
Office, at the Four Courts, this man's signature
written when he was quite old, at the foot of a
certain State document, and I never saw more
exquisite caligraphy. The characters are small,
regular, and of most delicate formation. When
Bingham came into the Province, O'Rourke had
been several times in rebellion, and had always

beaten the Government. Perrott was Viceroy at
this time, and O'Rourke at once made his submission to Perrott. He recognised the son of Henry
VIII as his lawful superior, and shaped his course
accordingly. Besides, he liked Perrott and Perrott
liked him. Perrott induced him to join in the
Composition of Connaught and lay down his
O'Rourkeship with all its sovereign privileges and
powers. Then he legally ceased to be a chieftain
and became only a great landlord. He retained a
great deal of Leitrim in his own hands, and received
fixed rents from the proprietors of the remainder.
When his friend Perrott departed, O'Rourke was
left face to face with Bingham whom he disliked
and despised. During the Armada winter he received and sheltered some Spanish sailors. The
Government demanded their surrender with the
intention of hanging them as they had hanged all
the rest. O'Rourke replied that it did not consist
with his honour as a gentleman or his dignity as a
prince to surrender men whom he had admitted to
the rites of hospitality. Bingham now, without
notice, collected his forces and fell upon him.
Bingham thought to surprise him in his castle on
the shores of Lough Gill, but as snow lay on the
ground, Bingham's people were seen, and in short
this swoop on Bingham's part came to nothing.
O'Rourke then went into rebellion, and as a pre-
liminary desired his sheriff to shift somewhere else

for an office. His eldest son was at the time a
student at Oxford. O'Rourke sent one of his
gentlemen, Charles Trevor, thither secretly. Young
O'Rourke, afterwards celebrated as Brian Ogue
of the Battle-Axes, ran away from Oxford in company with Trevor, and came home through Scotland
and Ulster. He immediately took the field as one
of his father's chief lieutenants. In this rebellion
O'Rourke stirred up North Connaught, and kindled
a fierce flame of war. He sent for all the wood-
kerne and bad subjects and licensed them to make
prey within the borders of Bingham's Presidency.
In reply to a letter from Perrott he said he would
be under the government of no man in Ireland save
the Viceroy. The Government sent commissioners
to treat with him—Judges and Bishops. O'Rourke
received them like a king. He did not stir from
his place to meet them or once remove his cap from
his head. He regarded himself as a sovereign prince
owning no superiors on earth save the Queen and
her Deputy. Eventually, Bingham having beaten
the North Connaught insurgents, invaded Breffney
or the Brenny, O'Rourke's country, in three divisions. O'Rourke's own feudatories revolted against
him, and the constable of his forces turned traitor
and joined Bingham. O'Rourke now went into the
north to his ally The McSweeny, Red Hugh's
foster father. Red Hugh himself was at this time
prisoner in Dublin Castle. McSweeny hardly

knowing how he was to deal with this extraordinary proud and haughty being, in the end surrendered to him his own chieftainship. O'Rourke would not be chieftain without exercising a chief's functions, and actually hanged some of McSweeny's own kinsmen. Eventually he went to Scotland to seek aid from some of the great Scotch nobles. He was there arrested by James VI, who in pursuit of some tortuous State policy sent him forward to London as a present to the Queen. He was brought before the Council, Cecil, Walsingham and the rest. The Council looked at their remarkable captive so long known to them by report, now seen at last in the flesh, and the captive looked at the Council, so long well known to him, man by man. He stood erect, not a joint bending in back or knee, with his hat on, as when at Dromahaire he received the Commissioners of the Viceroy, a captive but also a king. "Why don't you kneel?" asked one of the Council, when they began to recover from the curious dramatic influence of the nature of the situation. He spoke in Latin, a tongue almost as familiar as Irish to the elder generation of the Irish and Norman-Irish chiefs. "I am not so used." "Are you not used to kneel before pictures?" "Yes, of God's saints—between whom and *you* there is much difference."

Dismissed by the Council, he was a second time brought from the Tower to the Court of Queen's

Bench to be tried before a jury on the charge of high treason.

The indictment having been read and translated for his benefit, for he did not understand English, Brian refused to plead save on four conditions :—

(1.) The assistance of an advocate.

(2.) The affidavits forwarded out of Ireland to be put in my hands.

(3.) The presence and examination in court of the persons who swore the affidavits.

(4.) The Queen in person to preside as Judge at my trial.

The fellow with a barbarous insolence, writes Camden, refused to plead save on these conditions. The first three everyone will now agree to have been mere justice. In the fourth we see the well-known pride of the man, surely an honourable pride, self-respect of an admirable and even heroic sort. To no jury of the fat and greasy sort would he make his defence, but to his liege Sovereign. All those Irish princes in the midst of their most furious rebellions never denied that the Queen was their sovereign. They rebelled against her officers and presidents, such as Bingham, who came with their intolerable wrong-doings between them and their Queen. I am surprised that the Queen did not pardon him. She understood Ireland well enough to know that men might rebel against her officers and yet entertain feelings of loyalty and regard for herself.   In O'Rourke's case her mind seems to have been preoccupied by an outrageous slander. It was charged against him that he had dragged the Queen's picture at the heels of his war-horse, and that he had stood by and approved while his men thrust their battle-axes through it.   Bingham, mendacious as well as ferocious, sent this story to London.   Great attempts were made to get it proved, but not the slightest evidence of any sort or description in support of the charge could be discovered.   The nearest thing to evidence was the following :—An image of the Virgin Mary was discovered in his country, and an ultra-clever official *deemed* that this image might have been assumed by the chieftain to be the effigy of the Queen and might have been treated in the manner described. But he confesses, honest man, that there were no marks of thrustings or slashings upon it.   This was the nearest thing to evidence.

The charge was of course a vile slander.   No man of O'Rourke's type, indeed no Irish gentleman of the period, could have stooped to such low rascal insolence.

To O'Rourke's most reasonable demands the Chief Justice replied that they could not be granted, adding further that if he persisted in his refusal to plead, he would be obliged to consider the charge of high treason as proved, and proceed to pass sentence of death.

" You will do as you please," replied the prince.

The Chief Justice sentenced him to death. He was led from the court, and a few days afterwards beheaded at Tyburn. Such was the end of Brian of-the-Ramparts, the first cousin of Red Hugh. There is surely something very refreshing in this proud refusal of the O'Rourke to plead his cause before a hired brehon and a parcel of money-grubbing London shopkeepers. His own chief tenants charged with treason were judged by himself, or a court of his chieftains over which he presided. He would accept no lower tribunal for himself, though his head should roll for it.

O'Rourke's last recorded speech was also highly characteristic. At the time of his execution there was a very vile Irish ecclesiastic in London, Miler Magrath, Archbishop of Cashel, a most sordid and knavish creature, an awful devourer of Church property—a perfect glutton in that way. In the next generation Strafford compelled his sons and nephews to disgorge a great deal of it. This ecclesiastical rascal, seeing a fellow-countryman led to the scaffold, thought good to join the procession, and administer religious consolation, by the way, to the chieftain. O'Rourke looked askance at Miler, and for the last time unclosed his laconic lips.

" I think," said he, " thou art a Franciscan who hast broken thy vows."

Such was the exit of Brian of-the-Ramparts O'Rourke, the proudest man who walked upon the earth in his day.

He was succeeded by his son Brian of the Battle-axes, of whom more presently.   Brian of the Battle-axes fixed himself in the Iron Mountains, and thence waged truceless war with Bingham, beat Bingham, recovered his father's territory and did some considerable things in his day.   Indeed a foray on his territory by Bingham, wherein his milch cows were driven from his lawn (an intolerable insult) was the proximate cause of the Nine Years' War.

DON JUAN DE AQUILA: HERO OF KINSALE.

In the summer of 1602, Philip III, King of Spain, determined to send an army to the assistance of Tyrone and O'Donnell. The command of the expedition, which was limited to four thousand men, was offered in succession to several Spanish generals and was refused; they would not invade Ireland with less than eight thousand. Finally it was offered to Don Juan, who accepted. When he landed in Kinsale he had in fact only three thousand two hundred, a great many of them boys and raw recruits, whom he describes as beggars, and whom he had to teach how " to shoot out of a peece " after he landed. He had no cavalry.

Immediately on landing he published a proclamation, declaring that no civilian would be injured in person or property, and nothing taken from the people save at their own prices. All who desired it had leave to withdraw from Kinsale with their property; those who had previously fled were permitted to return, and remove their property without molestation. Non-combatants and private

property were never so treated in Ireland before.
Don Juan was the first military commander who
ever waged war in Ireland according to the rules
of modern civilized warfare. He never expected
that he could defend Kinsale against the Queen's
armies. It was a small town of about two hundred
houses, with walls of no defence against culverins,
however strong against battering rams, mantelets,
and the other rude contrivances of mediæval
engineers. It was open to battery from the sea,
and was dominated everywhere by neighbouring
heights. He just hoped that he might be able to
hold the place until the arrival of the northern lords,
should they march at once and march fast. Red
Hugh came at once with wings. Tyrone did not ;
he made a leisurely campaign in Meath, and returned home again, before he proceeded, still in
a leisurely manner, to move towards Kinsale. So
Don Juan was thrown quite on his own resources.
His defence of Kinsale for some three months
against great Royalist armies is the most brilliant
example of combined pluck, skill, and endurance
with which I am acquainted in Irish history. I
calculate that at least 15,000 men, not to mention
the Queen's fleet occupying the harbour and
bombarding thence, broke themselves against the
indomitable energy of this man, and his handful of
Spanish infantry, and *besognies* just taught how
"to shoot out of the peece." To keep out the

Queen's fleet he first seized the two keys of the harbour, Rincorran and Castle Park, and prepared them for the reception of his artillery, which was due, but which never came. To repel the land army he ran out trenches, and dug shelter-pits towards those points where the enemy would be likely to plant their cannon.

Now, on all sides, a vast assailing force converged upon him—the army of Ulster, under Captain Blayney; of Leinster, under the Marshal of Ireland; the veteran army of Connaught, all Irish, under Clanricarde; the army of Munster, under Carew; the gentlemen and feudal levy of West Cork and Kerry; the gentlemen and feudal levy of East Cork and Tipperary, and, in detachments of 2,000 each, 6,000 fresh soldiers out of England. The keys of the harbour, through no fault of Don Juan, were captured, and the Queen's fleet rode close to the walls of the town. Every day and almost every night there was fierce and desperate fighting between Don Juan's advanced parties and the Queen's people seeking to get closer and build their batteries. At the beginning Don Juan's soldiers, the *besognies*, I presume, were of opinion that as soon as they were fairly worsted they were at liberty to flee. Don Juan soon stopped this. He issued a military proclamation that every man who retreated before the enemy without being ordered to do so by his officer would be shot.

Under such a regime his boys, and besognies soon became first-class specimens of Spanish infantry. The Spanish infantry were the best in the world at that time, and Don Juan's men brought no stain upon the glory of the service. By the way, there was a Spanish-Irish detachment in Don Juan's army commanded by Don Dermutio and Don Carlo M'Cartie. The refugees fought as well as any.

Mountjoy, foiled in his efforts to get close to the walls, next determined on a universal bombardment, hoping to pulverize the little town by sheer weight of the metal flung into it. He planted a great battery on the spit of land at Castlepark, another at Knockrobin in the North, and other guns at different points of vantage, with well elevated muzzles. The Queen's warships too, under Admiral Levison, got ready, and there was a terrible bombardment continuing for several days, and a vast quantity of lead and iron was flung into the little town. But many of the houses were really urban castles, not to be broken by such small shot, and Don Juan's quick and versatile soldiery repaired rents and damages as fast as they were made. The bombardment sounded awful to the surrounding rustics—it was like the end of the world; but Don Juan did not mind it, though one shot came through the roof of his house and, I think, broke a tun of wine.

Mountjoy ordered the bombardment to cease, and made another effort to bring his huge culverins close to the town. It must be remembered that in all the fightings around Kinsale Don Juan was at a great disadvantage, having no cavalry, while Mountjoy was very strong in that arm. This time Mountjoy succeeded. He drew his culverins within "half a musket shot" of the North Gate, threw up the necessary defences in spite of all resistance, and pounded mightily upon the gateway. A great breach was made there, into which, when deemed assaultable, the army of Ulster was sent, and sent in vain. The Ulstermen, after two hours' attempting, were rolled back by the Spanish heroes. That night slow-moving Tyrone was within a few days' march of Kinsale. Hardly was the last shot fired at the North Port when Mountjoy sent 2,000 men westward with digging tools to make a battery near the West Port. Through the breach which he hoped to make here he designed to send the fiery young Clanricarde and the Connaught Irish : they, if any men in the army, were likely to do the business. All that night and all next day the diggers digged and the carpenters hammered, nailing down the platforms, though harassed by sallies and much firing from the walls and Spanish shelter pits. At night all was ready for the reception of the culverins. Next day the walls would be breached ; the day after the Connaught men would storm

through. Every hour was now important, for
Tyrone was very near. Night fell, "foule and
rainy" and "extreme dark." The Spaniards
seemed very quiet to-night. Silence reigned in
Kinsale from five o'clock till eight. At eight Don
Juan sallied with 2,000 men—his whole available
force—putting his whole strength into that blow.
The Spaniards carried all before them; tore asunder
the platforms, filled the trenches, and with "incredible fury," gave upon the old works too,
those fronting the North Gate. It is said that
in that fierce sally they would have carried the
camp also and utterly routed Mountjoy but for the
arrival of Clanricarde and the Connaught army,
who were stationed some distance to the west, and
marched promptly through the dark night following
the sound of the firing.

Next day Mountjoy turned his guns with their
muzzles away from Kinsale. Slow Tyrone was
now at hand. The siege of Kinsale was over. Don
Juan's work was done. In Spain, doubtless, no one
remembers him, but the genius of Irish history
absorbs affectionately the whole story of his heroic
defence of Kinsale against great odds. Spaniard
as he was, Don Juan is now one of the notables of
Irish history. He fought against great odds in a
most gallant manner, and was in other respects a
beautiful example of chivalry and courtesy.

Mountjoy got no fighting out of his English

soldiers. They were wretched material to begin with, pressed men and beggars and gaol-birds, and when they arrived at Kinsale either fell sick and died or ran away. They had no love of powder, and could not endure hardship. All the fighting was done by Irishmen. Mountjoy's great victory, the battle of Kinsale, was in fact won by young Clanrickarde and the Connaught Irish. This gallant young chieftain whose beauty was as remarkable as his gallantry, married the widow of Sir Philip Sidney, who was also the widow of Robert, Earl of Essex.

THE BATTLE OF THE CURLEW MOUNTAINS.

CHAPTER I.

CLIFFORD INVADES SLIGO.

IN treating of the fall of the Queen's favourite, Robert, Earl of Essex, historians have not at all sufficiently recognised his very bad record as Chief Governor of Ireland. They say he did nothing, but in fact he did a great deal less, for he was beaten by the insurgent lords at many points. As he marched through the Queen's County young O'More, lord of that region, routed his rear-guard and plundered his baggage in the Pass of Plumes. At Askeaton, Co. Limerick, he was beaten by the Geraldines and driven back out of West Munster. The sons of Feagh MacHugh defeated his cavalry in one battle and his infantry in another. Finally his lieutenant, Sir Conyers Clifford, President of Connaught, was first beaten by Red Hugh at Ballyshannon and afterwards beaten disastrously in the Curlew Mountains. With such an Irish record it is not surprising that on his return to London his reception should have been so cold. I propose here to give a sketch of this latter battle, partly to enable the reader to form some idea of the curiously embroiled and intertangled relations of the chieftainry with each other and with the State, and partly with the purpose of illustrating the war-methods of the sixteenth century as practised in Ireland.

When the " Nine Years' War " broke out Sir Richard Bingham was master of all Connaught. Presently he came into collision with Red Hugh, and Red Hugh beat him. Red Hugh was only a boy, yet he beat the veteran and shook most of Connaught loose from his control. When Essex came into Ireland, Bingham was hopelessly beaten and could hardly venture to show himself outside the gates of Athlone. The Burkes of Clanricarde and the O'Briens of Thomond, two zealous royalist clans, alone kept the Queen's flag flying in the open, and Red Hugh was destroying them. Then the Queen recalled Bingham in disgrace. He was brought to London as a state prisoner pursued by an infinity of complaints urged against him by chieftains of the West, and Sir Conyers Clifford appointed President of Connaught simultaneously with the appointment of the Earl of Essex as Lord Lieutenant of the realm. Clifford seems to have been a man of signal nobility of character. The Four Masters declare that '' there did not come of English blood into Ireland in the latter times a more worthy person." His reputation preceded him, and on his arrival a considerable proportion of the western lords who had been previously in rebellion and allies of Red Hugh waited upon him and tendered him their allegiance. So without striking a blow Clifford recovered immediately the greater portion of the Province. Then at the head of a considerable army he marched northwards for the invasion of Tyrconnel but did not succeed. Red Hugh beat him at Ballyshannon, drove him back and resumed his operations in Connaught.

The county of Sligo was one of the divisions of Connaught in which the change produced by the coming of Clifford was not felt. It was still strongly held by Red Hugh's lieutenants. In 1598 Clifford flung into that county a young Royalist chieftain and a body of horse with the object of exciting there a rebellion of Red Hugh's feudatories. A cavalry battle ensued in which the Royalists were overthrown by Red Hugh's horse, and the leader of this forlorn hope, in fact The O'Conor Sligo, was driven within the fortress of Collooney and there besieged by Red Hugh.

Partly to relieve him, partly to deliver another great stroke at Red Hugh, Clifford mustered his forces at Athlone. When all was in readiness Clifford rose thence and marched to Boyle, a strong town in the north of Roscommon, close to the frontiers of Sligo. Between Roscommon and Sligo lay the Curlew Mountains, on the north side of which all the country was held by Red Hugh, except Collooney, which he was blockading. Clifford's force numbered 2,500 infantry and 300 horse. It consisted of Connaught-Irish, Meath-Irish and regulars. The regulars were, for the most part Irish too, but officered to some extent by English gentlemen. The Connaught and Meath contingents represented the military quotas which those provinces were bound to furnish for war. On demand under certain conditions, all the nobles and landowners were bound to "rise out," as the phrase ran, at the head of a fixed body of foot and horse well equipped and serve at their own expense for forty days. To our notions Clifford's army on this occasion was absurdly small. But in the sixteenth century such a force was not small, but, on the contrary, a great host. The State was seldom able to put into the field for active service an army of more than 4,000 men, nor the insurgent chiefs one of greater dimensions. When at Kinsale the contending powers severally brought all their forces to a head, out of the whole of Ireland there were but some six or seven thousand effective men on each side.

At the head of this force Clifford, on the 13th of August, marched through the gates of Boyle in the midst of wild weather and heavy pouring rain. The army had come that day from the town of

Roscommon and entered Boyle wet and weary and thinking only of supper, rest, and sleep. Clifford took up his quarters in the monastery there, the rest of his army was billeted throughout the town. Monastery and town must have been of considerable capacity, for I find a little later a garrison of 1,500 men posted here. Clifford's army, I say, expected to sleep comfortably in Boyle that night, but they did not. Shortly after their arrival the army was on march again, moving silently through darkness and rain towards the Curlew Mountains. Why we shall see presently.

CHAPTER II.

NIAL GARF MOUNTS GUARD OVER COLLOONEY.

WHEN Red Hugh heard of this invasion he lay, with cavalry only, blockading the castle of Collooney. Within that castle was the O'Conor Sligo. Hugh was very anxious to lay his hands upon O'Conor Sligo who had, for a long time, given him a great deal of trouble. Hearing the tidings, Hugh wrote to Tyrone to come and help ; Tyrone came by forced marches, but was unable to help. He came too late. Hugh also sent the usual war summons to all his feudatories and captains, and

all these being near came to him at once. These
were O'Dogherty, the three M'Sweenies, O'Boyle,
O'Byrne, M'Clancy, O'Gallagher and others. His
army when assembled consisted of about 2,500
men, horse and foot. We see here a proof of Red
Hugh's military power. On the sudden he was able
to draw together a force as great as that of the
Queen's president of all Connaught. Nor was it
in any respect less efficient. Hugh now rose from
Collooney, but left behind him 200 horse to con-
tinue the blockade.

To the command of this force he appointed his
cousin, Nial Garf—i.e., Nial the Rough. I notice
him here particularly, for it was this rough cousin
whose defection a little afterwards broke Red
Hugh's brilliant career. Nial Garf rebelled
against Red Hugh, became the "Queen's"
O'Donnell and led a great Queen's party in the
north-west.

He was a violent, headstrong, implacable young
man, and most furious both in speech and demeanour.

As Hugh Roe with the bulk of his army marches
southwards from Collooney, imagine Nial Garf with
his 200 horsemen moving round that fortress
through the trees and Nial's fierce and strident
voice uplifted at times ringing out words of menace
and command. That young man, afterwards the
Queen's O'Donnell, was certainly the roughest,

ruggedest, and most bull-headed and bull-hearted creature to be found anywhere at this time. On the march Red Hugh detached a second force. This went to the town and harbour of Sligo. Why I shall now explain.

CHAPTER III.

THE LAND BURKE AND THE SEA BURKE.

THE large army with which Clifford marched to Boyle represented only one wing of his invasion. He was, in fact, invading Red Hugh's country by sea as well as by land. Amongst Clifford's Connaught allies was one noteworthy figure. Theabod Burke, son of Granuaile and of her second husband, Rickard-in-Iron, lord of all Mayo. Granuaile, I think, was still alive. A short time before this she had written to her friend, Queen Elizabeth, informing her that she had now quite done with war and was engaged '' in farming.'' I must mention, however, that at the same time Bingham also wrote to the Queen complaining that Granuaile, in spite of her great age, was the root of all the hurley-burleys and disturbances of the West of Ireland. '' Even in our ashes live our wonted fires.''

This Theabod was commonly called '' Theabod of the Ships,'' and said to have been borne by

Granuaile on the high seas while she was returning to Ireland from her famous visit to Queen Elizabeth. Both these termagants entertained for each other a kindly feeling. They kept up a correspondence, and it was ever friendly. There is no truth in the tradition that Granuaile affected any sort of equality with the Queen, though possibly enough she did refuse a countess-ship at the hands of Elizabeth which would have been only a white elephant to her in Connaught. At this time, " Theabod of the Ships " inherited his mother's authority over the brave seafaring nation of the O'Malleys. By law or by the strong hand he was Admiral of Connaught, and had armed galleys and sailors enough to support his claims. He was also pretender to the Northern MacWilliamship, that is to say, to the supreme Government of the great county of Mayo. He put forward this pretension in right of his father, Rickard-in-Iron, the late MacWilliam. In the beginning of the Nine Years' War Theabod had rebelled against Bingham and allied himself with Red Hugh, in fact all the MacWilliam Burkes of Mayo had rebelled on that occasion. Red Hugh marched into the county and held a great convention of all the Burkes with the purpose of appointing a new MacWilliam. Now the claimant who had the best right according to Irish law happened to be very old, whereas Hugh required a stout, active soldier to act as his lieutenant in Mayo. He accordingly chose as fittest for his purpose a youth known as Theabod son of Walter, and solemnly installed him as the new MacWilliam, passing over the claims Theabod, son of Granuaile. The latter Theabod accordingly rebelled against Red Hugh and joined Clifford. I may here observe that from this "Theabod of the Ships," son of Granuaile, sprang the Earls of Mayo, one of whom not long ago distinguished himself so much as Governor-General of India. Theabod also made a private treaty with the O'Conor Sligo and married his sister. When Clifford determined to invade Tir-Connall he resolved to utilise the services of this welcome ally. He intended upon this expedition to rebuild the great castle of Sligo which commanded the roads from the North into Connaught and which Red Hugh had recently dismantled. In obedience to Clifford's request Theabod brought all his ships to Galway and there loaded them with lime and timber, and building tools and materials of all kinds, taking also on board a great number of masons. This done he sailed round Connaught, put into the harbour of Sligo, and there cast anchor, waiting till Clifford and the invading land force should arrive. He would then disembark all his masons and materials.

Red Hugh accordingly as he marched south to the Curlews detached to Sligo that force of 400 men to keep a watch upon Theabod. Red Hugh prudently appointed to the command of this force a gentleman who was certain to do his very best upon Theabod. This was Hugh's new MacWilliam, the other Theabod, Theabod son of Walter. The reader, while other developments are coming, will keep in mind these two Burkes, the land Burke and the sea Burke glowering upon each other at Sligo, the sea Burke rocking idly on the blue waters of the bay, and the land Burke encamped about the ruins of the old castle observing the motions of his adversary, an adversary whom he regarded as a rebel against his just and legitimate authority, and whom if he could catch he would hang with the greatest pleasure. For the land Burke was the MacWilliam, and as such lord of every Burke in the north of Connaught, including the sea Burke. On the other hand the sea Burke who had been also nominated MacWilliam, regarded the land Burke with just the same feelings. For the present, however, they can do nothing but scowl at each other and hurl opprobrious expressions. It was like a war between a sword-fish and leopard.

CHAPTER IV.

RED HUGH BLOCKS THE CURLEWS.

HUGH ROE at the head of the rest of his army marched straight forward to the Curlews, going with his accustomed velocity and encamped on the northern slopes of the same. From Boyle two roads led through the mountains into Sligo. One of these was circuitous, rugged and easily defended. It was unlikely that Clifford would try to force the Curlews by this road, nevertheless Hugh blocked it with 300 picked men, pikes and guns, no cavalry. He himself leading the bulk of his forces, and a considerable body of churls bearing spades and axes advanced from his camp along the direct road till he came to the blackened ruins of a castle which once commanded a gorge on the southern slope of the mountains. This castle had been erected by Bingham both for the defence of the Pass and as a fetter on the warlike MacDermot clan who occupied this region. Shortly after the breaking out of the war it had been stormed and burnt by the chief of this clan, MacDermot of the Curlews, a brave man, not at all so rude and wild as one might imagine, as the reader will discover later on.

At this point Red Hugh determined to fight with Clifford, and to that end ordered the erection there of a barricade with double flanks. This was early on the morning of the 13th, and at the time when Clifford was marching out of Roscommon along the road to Boyle. The morning was bright and fine, but the atmosphere was suspiciously transparent. From the mouth of the gorge, through a small opening in the trees, the walls, towers, and turrets

of Boyle could be distinctly seen white and glisten-
ing in the sunlight. Red Hugh, who was on horse-
back, and surrounded by his chiefs and principal
officers, stood still for a while, and regarded it
intently. This young man, now for many years the
terror of all Royalists in the West, was only 26
years of age, and even looked younger than he was,
so clear and fresh was his complexion, so vivid his
countenance, so alert and rapid was he in all his
movements. Yet he was no boy, but already a
skilful commander in the field, and a strong and
resolute administrator. Then he bade his men fall
to, and the adjoining woods rang with the noise of
axes, and presently sounded with the crash of falling
timber. Meantime the gorge was alive with spade-
men labouring diligently under the directions of
the young chief's engineers, and gradually the
barricade began to assume form. Once for all, let
me warn the reader against the common and
ignorant notion that the armies of the insurgent
lords were rude crowds of what are vaguely known
as kerne. They were armies in the proper sense of
the word, armed, directed, and handled according
to the best military methods in vogue at the time.

Shortly after noon the sky became overcast, and
at two o'clock the rain fell, and continued to fall.
At four there was a sound of the firing of heavy
ordnance from the direction of Boyle; it was the
garrison of Boyle saluting the army of the Presi-

dent. The flashes were quite visible. Red Hugh believed that Clifford, after a short halt, would roll forward again, and force the passage of the Curlews. The probability also was that he would advance by the direct road. Should he prefer the more circuitous route, Hugh believed that the three hundred planted there would be able to retard his advance sufficiently to enable himself to transfer his army by the nearest cross country ways, and fight Clifford upon that road at a point which he had already settled in his mind. Clifford, in fact, was not aware that Red Hugh was in this neighbour-hood at all ; for Hugh had come from Collooney with extraordinary celerity. Clifford imagined that he had only to deal with MacDermot of the Curlews, Hugh's marcher-lord in this region. Behind the barricade Hugh's people stood under arms, the gunmen forward with matches already lit, behind them the battle, and on the wings kerne—i.e., light foot, armed only with swords and javelins. His few horsemen were posted under shelter of a wood on the right of the barricade. Presently the whole of Clifford's army reached Boyle, and instead of advancing, as Red Hugh firmly expected, entered Boyle, presumably for a short rest and for refresh-ment. Now, however, hour succeeded hour, and there was no sign of the emergence of Clifford's people from Boyle. On the contrary, as night fell, Hugh's scouts came in with intelligence that all the bugle notes heard in the town indicated that the Royalist army would pass the night there. The rain now began to fall in torrents, and the wind rose to a storm howling in the forest, and whistling round the crags of the mountain sides. It grew dark two hours before darkness was due. Red Hugh now determined to lead his army back to camp, leaving a force of gunmen to hold the barricade as well as they could in the event of a night attack. Such an attack might possibly be delivered, but was he to keep his army here all night under arms waiting for an assault which might never come? In that event his tired men would have to contend in the morning with Clifford's well rested and refreshed forces. Hugh was himself full of strategy, and tactical wiles and guiles, renowned for the suddenness of his onfalls and the celerity of his movements. He did not credit Royalist commanders with a talent for the execution of such strokes, and rightly. The Queen's armies, for reasons into which we need not now enquire, were slow in their movements, and their action could, as a rule, be predicted. Hugh bade the officer in charge of the barricade send a swift mounted messenger to him at the first sign of the approach of Clifford's men, bade the bugles sound retreat, and rode away with his army, winding darkling through the wild Curlews.

CHAPTER V.

THE QUEEN'S MCSWEENY.

RED HUGH did not succeed in bringing all his soldiers back to camp. Shortly after that sounding of the trumpets, there emerged from the woods on the right side of the barricade three men wearing brazen morions, two with guns on their shoulders, who stepped down the slope swiftly, going in the direction of Boyle. The man who had no gun was a gentleman of the McSweeny nation. His name is unknown, but his purpose is well known. He was about to change sides and ally himself with the cause of the Queen. He believed that his change of sides would be peculiarly welcome to the Queen's people just now, because he brought with him important intelligence. He could tell them that the narrow gorge at the head of the Curlew Pass was undefended, that Hugh Roe, trusting to the blackness and wetness of the night, had marched back to camp, and that if they wished to do a good stroke upon him, now was the time.

No one can study the history of Elizabethan Ireland without being amazed and disgusted at the choppings and changings which marked the careers of nearly all the chieftains. Granuaile's son fought first for Hugh Roe and then for the Queen, and changed sides twice after that. His rival, the land Burke, now with Hugh Roe, was once a pillar of the Queen's cause in Mayo. Red Hugh himself, once the Queen's O'Donnell and her sworn ally, is now in rebellion. His cousin Nial Garf, now in rebellion, will one day be a pillar of the Queen's cause in the north-west, and before the end of the war will be in rebellion again. O'Conor Sligo, now as a Queen's man blockaded in Collooney will presently be Red Hugh's man and in a year or two be a Queen's man again, so that Red Hugh will have to seize and imprison him and give his lordship to his brother. But in each case there is an explanation, and if one looks closely into the explanation one does not find the apparent treacheries so very surprising.

As for the deserters now stepping down the slopes of the Curlews, making for Boyle, whose red lights show through the darkness and the rain—why are they changing sides? The explanation is this:— Shortly after Hugh Roe arrived at the chieftainship, his foster father, McSweeny of the Battle-Axes, died. There were two candidates for that chieftainship, the son of Hugh's foster father, and the son of a former McSweeny, who was one of the most famous chieftains of his day, Murrough the Slow, a man grandly eulogized by the Four

Masters. The name of the latter candidate was Miler McSweeny, and of the two, I believe he had the better right, according to Irish law and custom. But the custom being so often broken by the strong hand, was not paramount, and so Red Hugh manfully stood by his own foster-brother and made him McSweeny of the Battle-Axes. He himself, Hugh Roe, was not O'Donnell by Irish law. There were others who had better claims. He was O'Donnell partly by the strong hand, and partly by Royal favour, for he began his career as the Queen's O'Donnell. He had, therefore, naturally, no superstitious reverence for Irish law and custom which enjoined that the eldest of the clan regnant, whether nephew, son, uncle or cousin, should succeed to a vacant chieftainship. Accordingly, Hugh Roe made his foster-brother the McSweeny, and passed over Miler, son of Murrough the Slow. Miler, collecting his most faithful followers and kinsmen, rebelled, was beaten, and fled out of Tir-Connall. He and his then enlisted in the service of the Queen. The authorities promised him that after the overthrow of the usurping Hugh Roe, he should be McSweeny of the Battle-Axes. So he became a Queen's man heart and soul. He was with Essex in the Munster campaigns, and so distinguished himself there for valour and conduct that Essex knighted him. He was now Sir Miler

McSweeny, and one of the celebrated soldiers of the day. He had recently come from Munster into Connaught. He was a close friend of Sir Conyers Clifford, the President, and was, I believe, captain of his life-guard. Sir Miler McSweeny is now marching northwards, hoping to overthrow Red Hugh, to drive out the usurping McSweeny, and to rule in his stead over the lordship of which he had been so tyrannously deprived. The three men whom we saw deserting Red Hugh are ancient friends or kinsmen of Sir Miler. Learning that he was so near, they resolved to take advantage of the darkness and rain, and join him in Boyle. No doubt they loved Sir Miler, and probably enough, like many soldiers, had various grounds of complaint against their own commander.

So these three men stepped from the slopes of the Curlews, crossed the dark wet plain, presented themselves to the sentinels at Boyle, and were led into Sir Miler's presence. To him they explained the situation. By him it was also explained to Sir Conyers and his officers, with the result that in a short time the bugles rang out, and all Boyle sounded with the noise of military preparation. In spite of darkness and teeming rain, Clifford's army got on march again, and rolled forward through the night towards the pass in the Curlew mountains, which, as we know, was now practically undefended.

CHAPTER VI.

BRIAN OGUE OF THE BATTLE-AXES.

WHEN Hugh Roe arrived at his camp he found himself reinforced by the arrival of the lord of Leitrim, The O'Rourke, Brian Ogue of the Battle-Axes. It was he whose milch cows Bingham had seized upon the lawn at Dromahaire. It was he who, by exacting vengeance on the Binghams for that insult, had unintentionally kindled all the North into rebellion, and so precipitated the Nine Years' War. He arrived in camp leading a little army of horse and foot, and amongst the foot 160 big gallowglasses clad in shirts of glittering chain-mail, and carrying long battle-axes. As these gallow-glasses played a great part in the Battle of the Curlew Mountains, the reader must not forget them. Brian Ogue came late, and in fact till the last moment had some notion of not coming at all. If it be asked whether Brian Ogue's record as an insurgent was fair, clear, and consistent, I must reply that it was not. He, too, hovered from side to side. The explanation of Brian Ogue's vacillations is interesting in itself, and will help to illustrate the character of the times.

Brian Ogue was his father's eldest son, but his mother and father separated. He was the son of

Brian of-the-Ramparts, that inordinately proud
chieftain of Breffney.

Subsequently Brian Ogue's father married the
Lady Mary Burke, sister of Ulick, Earl of Clanricarde. I would have the reader remember that
there was little or no difference between great
people in Ireland and great people in England and
elsewhere at this time. They were essentially the
same class. So we find that while Brian of-the-
Ramparts married one sister of Ulick, the Earl,
Sir Henry Malby, the Queen's President of
Connaught, married another. Again, the eldest
son of Ulick married the Lady Frances Walsingham, who was widow of Sir Philip Sidney, and also
of Robert, Earl of Essex. So this high lady, one
of the highest in the Empire, called Brian of-the-
Ramparts O'Rourke " uncle." They were all
essentially the same sort of people, and recognised
each other as such.

The Lady Mary Burke bore a son to O'Rourke.
He was called Cathal. When O'Rourke went
into rebellion Cathal was a child. So, for purposes
of war and government, he had to lean on his eldest
son, Brian Ogue. Consequently, when the old
O'Rourke was executed for treason, Brian Ogue
of the Battle Axes succeeded him as chieftain.
Meantime, Lady O'Rourke sent her boy to school
to Limerick, where he was put under the care of a
certain Master White, who kept a large school

there, frequented by the sons of the western and southern lords. The Government kept an attentive eye upon that school. When boys were removed in large numbers it was a storm-signal. It meant that their fathers were going into rebellion. The reader will now see that though Brian Ogue of the Battle Axes was lord *de facto* of Leitrim, his half-brother, the school-boy, being his father's eldest legitimate son, was lord *de jure*. Brian Ogue had in fact, no claim whatsoever to that chieftainship, save the right of the strong hand. When Clifford came into the province Brian Ogue intrigued with him. He hoped that Clifford in return for military assistance would be able to establish him in his insecure lordship and strike some arrangement between himself and the house of Clanrickarde which, of course, supported the title of their kinsman the boy Cathal. In fact Brian Ogue about this time would have openly sided with the Queen and supported Clifford to the utmost of his power but for the menaces of Red Hugh. Red Hugh had to flash his sword, so to speak, several times in the eyes of Brian Ogue before he could deter him from that course.

Though Brian Ogue now came late to Red Hugh's hosting he did come and his arrival was very welcome to Red Hugh. This Brian, as we have seen elsewhere, was an Oxford man. He was at the University when his father went into rebellion. Hearing the news he fled from Oxford and came home through Scotland and Ulster.

Hugh marching south to the Curlews left no enemy behind him. Ballymote, the third great fortress of the territory, had fallen into his hands in the previous year. It was the capital, as one might say, of the barony of Corran, the lord of which barony was a MacDonough.

In the previous year this MacDonough of Corran captured Ballymote from the O'Conor Sligo and drove out the Queen's people. He then sold Ballymote to Red Hugh, after which it became Hugh's headquarters. This event, as recorded in the *Four Masters,* is curiously suggestive of the times : —

" The Governor of Connaught and O'Donnell, i.e., Red Hugh, were bidding against each other for the castle and proposing to purchase it from the MacDonoughs. But the end of the matter was that the MacDonough gave the castle to O'Donnell on terms of purchase and contract in the middle month of the harvest of this year. £400 and 300 cows was the price which O'Donnell gave the MacDonoughs for the town."

Here then we see a powerful chieftain affecting neither cause, but anxious only to make the most he could out of the situation. But to judge any of

Note.—It may interest the reader to know that Ballymote was the home of the Taafe family, now for a long time very powerful in Austria. When the Nine Years' War came to an end Ballymote was granted to the Taafes who were created Viscounts of Corran. They fought for the Crown against the Puritans, were expelled, and went into the Austrian service.

these men, we must get out of the nineteenth century and take our stand in the midst of the sixteenth, and that, indeed, is not easy.

CHAPTER VII.

RED HUGH GIVES HIS MEN A GOOD BREAKFAST AND A SHORT SPEECH.

Now drew on the Feast of the Virgin Mary, a festival still known among our peasantry as Lady Day in harvest. On the day before the feast Red Hugh proclaimed a solemn fast. All fasted, confessed and " received the Body of Christ," and went to bed hungry but comforted. All the confederated chieftains gave themselves out as champions of the Church. Policy if not principle led to the adoption of that course. The assumption of such a rôle would give them greater power over their followers, and enable them to draw support from the Catholic princes of the Continent. The religious question, however, had, I think, very little to do with this or any of the Irish wars of the sixteenth century. The princes of Ireland really fought in defence of their feudal independence. Born kings, and educated under all the old dynastic influences, they could not brook the huge invasions which the advance of the central authority during this century made upon their privileges—the tax-gatherers, the sheriffs, the Provincial Presidents, the going judges of Assize, the abolition of cuttings and spendings, of suppers and cosherings, etc. The Queen's Irish were all Catholics too, and I suppose quite as devout. But the confederate chiefs, for one reason or another, were wont to represent themselves in a peculiar degree as champions of the Church. So Red Hugh solemnly proclaimed a fast on the eve of Lady Day, after which he and his warriors went to bed hungry but comforted.

Hugh took good care of his men. They were protected from the weather and from ague and rheumatism by good leathern tents.[1] Hence we may presume that such a successful campaigner and swift journeyer looked well also to his commissiariat, and that his men lacked nothing which fighting men should have. Night fell, and also rain. Whoever waked that night heard it loud-pattering against the leathern walls, provoking thoughts.

It was the eve of the day of battle. All expected that Clifford would attempt to force the pass on the morrow. Some did not sleep and could not— viz., Red Hugh's scouts and sentinels keeping watch up the pass looking Boyle-ward from the

Historia Hiberniæ, p. 210.

bristly barricade, wet to the bone, but vigilant, peering through the darkness, or listening with inclined heads.

Morning dawned, still teeming, rain, rain, the heavy black sky promising an abundant downfall. Red Hugh looked out, and in his red head arose the conviction that the President would not move this day, would, on the contrary, remain comfortably in monastic Boyle. In gunmen the President was superior. Apart from natural disinclination to march and fight under such very pluvious conditions, he would be unwilling, thought Hugh, to neutralize his firearms. In those days of tow-matches and matchlocks the gunman was helpless before rain. Brave Hugh, too, I suppose, had little stomach for a wet day's fighting, and the fasting of the previous day, perhaps, made him less alert than usual, and helped the wish to engender the thought that Clifford would not stir, and that this, the Virgin's own day, would be spent in peace and festivity. His captains came and received their orders, not murmuring, whatever they may have thought, " for truly whatever he ordered it should be done according, as he commanded it by the word of his mouth.[2]

In social hours the young chieftain was gentle, but in all that related to war and government most

imperative and masterful. His captains departed,
and Red Hugh's camp gave no sign of an early
arming and preparation. But now arrived visitors
of a different sort. Horsemen galloped up to the
great central tent, and springing swiftly from the
saddle, announced that the enemy was on the
march, and, at their ease, crossing or about to
cross the strewn timber. The battle would not now
be fought where the advantage was with the
northerns, but on this side of the selected point and
on even terms. A swift shadow crossed the face
of the young prince at these ill tidings. Had he
known that this blow came from his own revolted
vassal, Sir Miler, it would probably have been
deeper. But quickly recovering himself he invented
new plans and sent out new orders. "Breakfast
at once for the whole army," was the first of these ;
surely a good beginning for a day which promised
to be one of long and continued battle. Breakfast,
too, was doubly necessary this morning, for his
devout warriors were hungry enough after
yesterday's severe abstinence. The ordinary fare
of Irish soldiers in this century was oat-meal or oat-
cake and butter, with milk. I have seen a contract
made between Hugh and one of his captains, very
precise about meal and money, but with no allusion
to meat. If the reader be not too anxious to get
on to the battle, perhaps the following Homeric
picture of the interior of an Irish camp at night,

and of the supper served round to the guards of
a 16th century Irish chieftain may not be unwel-
come : —[3]

" When Calvach heard that Shane had advanced
to that place with his forces he sent two of his
faithful men to reconnoitre them, whose names
were Donough Ogue, son of Donough Roe Maguire
and Maurice MacAilin. Those twain went forward
unnoticed until they were in the midst of the
warriors of Shane, who were so numerous that they
could not know one another even by day save only
by recognising their leaders.

" Those two just-mentioned persons moved on
from one camp-fire to another, till they came to the
great central fire which was in front of the tent-
door of the son of O'Neill, from which an immense
light blazed forth, for here in the centre was the
commander himself, and around that fire were sixty
war-like gallowglasses ready for action, with their
sharp, well-mounted battle-axes, and sixty resolute
determined Scots, with their broad, weighty, sore-
smiting swords in their hands, watching and
guarding the son of O'Neill.

" When the time arrived for the forces to take
their food, and while it was divided and distributed
among them, these two spies extended their hands
for their portion, like the rest, to the distributor,

[3] *Four Masters,* A D. 1557.

and what they received was their helmets full of meal, with a due proportion of butter.

"With these proofs they returned to their people. That night Shane was attacked, his army destroyed, and he himself barely escaped. In the division of the booty there fell to the share of Con, son of Calvach, the splendid steed of the son of O'Neill, which was called Mac-an-ilar, son of the eagle."

Red Hugh's warriors on this eventful morning got some such breakfast,[4] with milk. Meat probably, was added as far as possible. The prince surely gave his men as good a breakfast as his commissariat could supply.

Meantime he sent for one of his best officers, MacDermot of the Curlews, his marcher lord in this region, also for his own foster-brother, MacSweeny of the Battle-Axes, and for two brothers of the warlike and famous sept of the O'Gallaghers— namely, Eocha and Tully O'Gallagher. These he directed to take six standards of foot, gunmen for the most part, to advance into the mountains and gall and impede Clifford, all they could, in his progress through the Curlews ; and he appointed Mac Dermot chief in command. He also ordered Brian Ogue of the Battle-Axes to follow MacDermot

---

[4] " Extemplo jubet O'Donnellus milites cito capere cibum quo firmiores praeliando sint." Forthwith O'Donnell directs his soldiers to eat breakfast in order that they may be stronger for fighting.—Philip O'Sullivan.

with his 160 heavy-armed Breffneian gallowglasses, as a solid back to that skirmishing party. These captains having received their orders, returned to their quarters and made the necessary preparations. Breakfast now over, Red Hugh appeared in armour before his tent, where the army was summoned to attend, and delivered a brief military harangue. He was now 26 years of age, had been for seven years prince of Tir-Connall, and had enjoyed seven years of almost unbroken triumph in war. The speech has been preserved by Philip O'Sullivan, who was personally acquainted with many who heard it. See *Historia Hiberniæ,* p. 210. In striving to imagine this scene, the reader will remember that Red Hugh was a very handsome youth. " His countenance," say the veracious Four Masters, who knew him, " was so beautiful, that every one who looked upon him, loved him." He was perfectly proportioned, very strong, and well set in figure, of middle height, rather tall than short. His complexion was of that clear brightness which usually accompanies red hair, and his eyes, full, gray, and luminous, and keen as an eagle's.

" Soldiers, through the help of the Holy Virgin, Mother of God, we have ere this, at all times conquered our heretic foe. To-day we will annihilate him. In her name yesterday we fasted. To-day we celebrate her feast. So then in the Virgin's name, let us bravely fight and conquer her enemies."

Shouts and the clash of arms proved that he had touched the right chord in the hearts of those simple warriors, for whom the middle ages had by no means passed away, but who were still as devout, and in the old way, as their forefathers of the days of the Crusaders.

With banners waving, war-pipes screaming, MacDermot and his 600 marched swiftly into the mountains. Rain still fell, but not heavily. After him, at a slower pace, followed Brian Ogue and his mailed gallowglasses, over whom waved the O'Rourke banner, showing the lions of the house of Breffney surmounted by a mailed hand grasping a dagger. As MacDermot and Brian Ogue disappeared, folded away and hidden in the hollows of the hills, Red Hugh and his host also advanced till they reached a point at which Clifford's progress might best be obstructed.[5] The point selected by Red Hugh for fighting the battle of the Curlew Mountains was one where cavalry could not operate, and where his flanks could not be turned. He sent his war-horses to the rear and dismounted

---

[5] The name of this place was, Dunaveeragh. In one account of Red Hugh's speech, he is represented as concluding with these words—" The congregation at the altar will make way for you, murmuring, ' This is a man who fought at Dunaveeragh.' "

his lancers, for he was resolved to put his whole strength into the contest at this selected point. Here he was rejoined by the 300 whom he had previously planted as a guard upon that unused and circuitous road, and where their presence was no longer necessary. Having made all his dispositions, he and his chief officers rode forward in the track of MacDermot and Brian Ogue, to see how matters fared in the hills, whence probably sounds of firing already came.

Red Hugh expected that he would be soon rejoined by his skirmishers falling back before Clifford's advance.

CHAPTER VIII.

CLIFFORD ENTERS THE CURLEWS.

To return to Clifford. The three deserting McSweenies arriving at Boyle informed their dear lord, Sir Miler, that the Curlews were undefended, Hugh Roe having marched back to camp. Sir Miler brought the news to Clifford. Clifford sent out the necessary orders, and presently all Boyle rang with the sound of bugles and the noise of military preparation. The tired soldiers had to buckle on their war-gear again and face once more the raging elements.

Soon the whole army, horse, foot, and carriages were again upon the road. The walls and turrets of monastic Boyle were left behind and Clifford's host rolled along the great road leading into Ulster across the Curlews, men and horses plodding wearily forward through the miry ways and driving rain. Clifford, by Sir Miler's advice, avoided the unfrequented way which Red Hugh had beset with 300 men. At the foot of the Curlews he bade Markham halt with the horse in a green pasture. Day now dawned, not rosy-fingered, but wet exceedingly.

It was about this time that at the other side of the Curlew Mountains the conviction arose in a certain red head there that Clifford would not march that day. The army now began to ascend the Curlews in three divisions. The vanguard was commanded by Sir Alexander Ratcliffe, son of the Earl of Sussex, the battle—i.e., the strong central division by Clifford himself. The rear-guard was brought up under Sir Arthur Savage, captain of a Norman-Irish nation of the county of Down.

About a quarter of a mile from the mouth of the passage Ratcliffe came upon "a barricado with doble flänckes," in fact the woody obstruction at which Red Hugh had intended to dispute the passage of the Curlews.* There were a few sentries there who discharged their muskets and fled. The place was practically undefended. Opening a passage through the barricado Sir Conyers placed guards upon the same with instructions not to stir until they should hear from him again, which they never did. On the right flank of the half-ript barricado he put Lieutenant Rogers and his company, on the left Ralph Constable, an officer held in high and deserved honour " for his virtue." Not far from Constable and on the same flank he posted Captain Walter Flood and Captain Windsor. Each of these captains had 40 men. There were 160 in all, Ralph Constable being chief in command. Should the army suffer a disaster in the mountains the Governor believed that Constable would hold the half barricaded gap and check the onrush of the pursuers. He was a prudent general and looked behind as well as before.

Having made these sensible arrangements, Clifford led his army into the heart of the Curlews. The Curlews are not so much mountains as great bleak highlands of a boggy character like nearly all Irish highlands and hills, a fact which accounts for

* Sir John Harrington in one of his letters says that on his return to England he will hold his own with any of the loudest captains and talk as well as he about barricadoes, cazemets, etc., etc., and truly in the Irish journal which he kept there is a bewildering maze of uncouth military phraseology thrown in I believe with humorous intent.

the softness and rounded beauty of our mountain scenery. Presently, still ascending, the army came upon a great expanse of brown moorland looked down on by distant hills. A grey road traversed the bog and at the further end stopped short suddenly in a green wood. The wood blocked the view northwards. Clifford could not tell what was going on at the other side of that wood. The road was not straight but swerved considerably, resembling a well bent bow. It was bordered by some ground moderately firm, studded with yellow furze whence its name Bohar-boy or the Yellow Road. As string to this bent bow there ran straight across the bog a sort of causeway, not exactly a way, but more of the nature of firm ground, rough and obstructed. Its course was traceable by the eye, for it was greener than the surrounding bog. This causeway leaving the regular road at a certain point north of the barricado fell in again with the road well on this side of the wood ; let the reader remember this rough causeway intersecting the bend of the road.

The army went by the road advancing as before in three separate divisions. Sir Alexander Ratcliffe was in the van, Clifford in the battle, Sir Arthur Savage leading the rear column. Carts and horses, mules and garrans bearing panniers filled the spaces between the columns. Here in fact went the baggage, ammunition, and provisions.

CHAPTER IX.

RATCLIFFE CLEARS THE BOHAR-BOY WOOD.

So over the vast brown bog the Royalist army, minus the cavalry, wound its way slowly towards the wood. Below them lay Constable and his 160 men guarding the barricado. Below these, again, Clifford's cavalry took their ease at the foot of the hills southwards. The passage of the Curlews was not yet achieved nor a point reached at which horse could be anything but a danger and encumbrance.

It was now morning. The pouring rain of the previous night gradually ceased, the sky cleared and the sun rose. The peasantry who from the hills watched the army saw the glittering of armour and weapons with thoughts friendly or hostile as the Queen's host slowly threaded the brown bog curving round towards the wood where all believed that the battle of the Curlew Mountains would now be lost or won.

As the atmosphere cleared the picturesqueness of the scenery became observable, lit up now in the light of the rising sun. Hills stood well defined against the blue of the sky. Bits of primeval forest showed here and there. The heather which still clothes these mountain sides was purpling with the advance of autumn, but had not yet assumed its deepest hues. Swollen by last night's pouring rain mountain streams flashed white in the distance. The Curlew Mountains, however, though picturesque, are not imposing and hardly deserve the name.

Such was the scene amid which the Queen's host advanced curving round by that bent road and approaching the wood which bounded the vast brown bog on the north. Flocks of flying curlews, scared by the sound and glitter, rose here and there, settling down at greater distances. All eyes were now fixed on the wood. It was obviously the next point, and Sir Conyers thought the last point at which the passage of the Curlews could be disputed with any advantage to the northerns.

All believed that this wood was filled with Red Hugh's warriors, and that the battle would be fought amid its depths. It was August 14th, and here as elsewhere autumn was laying a fiery finger on the leaves, upon the mountain ash chiefly, a tree very common in primeval Irish woods—also the first which yields itself to autumnal painting. Nor were Clifford's conjectures quite wrong, though too far from quite right. As Ratcliffe approached the wood the still quiet groves of it became suddenly alive. From some half thousand matchlocks scattered along its edge, each gunman there posted well behind a protecting tree, tongues

of fire flashed out through the leaves and scrub.
bullets of lead and iron began to rain into Ratcliffe,
and smoke concealed all greenery. Hoarse voices
in Gaelic shouted words of command, for here was
The MacDermot with Red Hugh's 600 arquebus
men, archers, and musketeers. The battle of the
Curlew Mountains had begun.

Forthwith Radcliffe formed his column for attack,
light troops forward, gallowglasses behind, and
plunged into the smoke regardless of the fast-
flashing tongues and the raining bullets. The firing
suddenly ceased. If there was any fighting it was
mostly hand-to-hand and unseen amid the trees. I
believe there was not much. As bold Ratcliffe and
his men with a shout plunged into and through the
wood, firing as they went, MacDermot and his
men began to pour out at the other side.

Although the wood might have been successfully
maintained had Red Hugh concentrated all his
forces there in time, it was not maintainable by
such strength as MacDermot had at his command.
I may mention here casually that Boyle had been
the capital of the MacDermot nation till fierce
Bingham took it from them, and, the Queen being
agreeable, conferred it upon himself, and that the
Monastery was a foundation of the same family. So
MacDermot had in this war something to fight for
beyond glory. MacDermot, however, could not
hold the wood. He fell back, he and his gunmen,

retreating upon Brian Ogue, who also with his
gallowglasses fell back northwards and nearer to
Red Hugh's camp, far enough, at least, not to
subject themselves to any very deadly fire on the
part of Ratcliffe's men, who now emerged, cheer-
ing, on the northern borders of the same, probably
sending thence a volley by way of military farewell
into The MacDermot's rear.   Ratcliffe had cleared
out the Bohar-boy wood in fine style, opening up,
so far, the passage of the Curlews. From the wood,
which was half a mile in depth, the road still running
northwards and Collooney-wards, now traversed
another brown bog, and along this moving off
leisurely and in good order Ratcliffe saw Mac
Dermot and the expelled gunmen retreating in the
wake of Brian Ogue of the Battle-Axes and his
small but formidable-looking cohort of mailed
gallowglasses trailing their long battle-axes.
Beaten so far were the northern, but obviously not
beaten to flight. Genial Homer would have pictured
MacDermot and Brian Ogue as two raw-devouring
lions beaten off from the cattle fold, but retreating
slowly, looking around and askance, not being at
all terrified in their minds. In such wise did Brian
Ogue of the long-shadowed battle-axe and
MacDermot of the loud war-cry yield before to
the fierce onrush of the Mac-an-Iarla.*

* Ratcliffe was son of the Earl of Sussex. The Irish at
this time had a great respect for Mac-an-Iarlas.

CHAPTER X.

BUT FINDS THAT THE BOG MUST BE FOUGHT FOR.

As soon as Clifford learned that Red Hugh's people had been driven out of the wood and that the way was cleared, he despatched a messenger with orders to Markham to bring up the horse. He, the messenger, aide-de-camp as we would now say, rode along the curving road through the first bog past Ralph Constable and his detachment who guarded the barricado, communicating to them the glad news, and so fared downwards and southwards to that green pasture, where the horses were grazing and the men were strolling about or sitting on their big military saddles, the ground being so wet.

But we must hasten back to more exciting scenes, noting only that at this time Markham and the Queen's horse began to get under way. Meantime the invading army was traversing the dangerous Bohar-boy wood which had been so gallantly cleared by Ratcliffe and the vanguard.

Here for half a mile the solid slow wheels groaned and screeched and the tramp of marching men echoed in the dim depths of the forest, intermingled with the sharper noise of the hoofs of horses, "and the trees waved above them their green leaves" sparsely touched with fire and gold "dewy with nature's tear-drops as they passed." Through this half-mile of primeval forest rolled the army, a scene of sylvan loveliness and beauty through which Destiny had determined that it should roll again not so harmoniously. Savage and the rear guard were probably still among the trees when the sound of fresh firing in front proved that Ratcliffe and the van were again engaged with the enemy, opening up a mile or two more of the wild road through the Curlews. The army as it emerged from the wood observed the same order of advance. Ratcliffe with his gunmen and light troops still in the van. The road now traversed another bog, bare too, save that there was on the eastern side, that to Ratcliffe's right, another wood lying rather further than a calyver's shot from the road. Upon this road MacDermot's men were still in view and also as Ratcliffe soon perceived deploying for fight, "not being at all terrified in their minds." The left wing of MacDermot's little army abutted on and was protected by the wood. His right leaned upon the hill side, for the road at this point skirted the mountain. The bog-plain sloped from right to left. MacDermot's right so leaned upon high and rugged ground, and his left upon the wood, a necessary arrangement, seeing that otherwise he, being of inferior strength, would be out-flanked and compelled to retreat even without shot fired. The ground upon which MacDermot deployed, though described as bog, was yet notwithstanding consistent enough for fighting purposes. Ratcliffe also drew out his men and disposed them in fighting order. There was no opportunity for manœuvering or nice feats of generalship It was a fair and even duel between the gunmen of both armies. Mac Dermot's men had the advantage of the ground, for they were more inured to fighting in such an element than regular troops. Ratcliffe's, on the other hand, were superior in numbers and furnished probably with a better style of weapon. Moreover, MacDermot's six hundred were not all gunmen. With them were interspersed bowmen, Scots for the most part, Red Hugh's maternal kindred, and javelin-men who hurled their spears exactly like the warriors of the Iliad, casting with great force and accuracy to an extraordinary distance. Remember, too, that Elizabethan fire-arms were very different towards ours. Good armour could resist the impact of their bullets and their range was very short. So javelin-men, Homeric spear-casters, trained from childhood to the practice of the art, were of considerable service when the opposing ranks come into some relative nearness.

Behind Ratcliffe's fast deploying men the rest of the Royalist army stood " refused," waiting till he should disperse this obstruction and clear the way once more. Immediately behind him was the first division of the convoy, then the main battle under the President, then the second convoy, after which Savage and the rear guard still struggling through the Bohar-boy wood.

CHAPTER XI.

FIGHT ON THE BOG SIDE.

IT was eleven of the clock, a clear and bright forenoon, all nature well washed and glittering from the heavy rainfall of the preceding night.

Now began in right earnest the conflict which is called the Battle of the Curlew Mountains. Many a battle had been fought upon this famous road as far back as the bright semi-fabulous epoch of Queen Maeve, and far beyond. By this road Ulster invaded Connaught, and Connaught, Ulster. Here defenders had the advantage, and many a fierce conflict had been fought and won upon these brown bogs. The great John de Courcy, and his ally, Cathal Red-Hand,* passed this way to fight William Fitz Adelm de Burgh, patriarch of all the

* " Cahal Mor, of the Wine-Red Hand, into whose heart God hath breathed more piety and virtue than into any of the Irish of his time."—*Four Masters.*

Irish Burkes. By this road, too, a son of the Red
Hand, fleeing before the face of the children of
William, once lifted all his people bodily out of
Connaught, seeking shelter with Red Hugh's ancestors. Many a famous march and battle had
been enacted in these celebrated mountains, which
now for the first time rang with the thunder of
modern weapons of war. So the descriptive energy
of our Four Masters is not quite so redundant and
uncalled for as we might imagine, when they pause
in their Annals to supply a picture of this new form
of martial terror : —

"As to the vanguard "—Ratcliffe's gunmen—
"they kept on advancing till they met the foreign
battalions," Red Hugh's Tir-Connallians under
MacDermot. "When they came close together,
MacDermot's men cast forth at them a destructive
pouring rain of their well-shaped ashen spears ;
flights of sharp-pointed arrows shot from their long,
strong and effective bows, and thick volleys of red
flaming flashes and of hot fiery balls of lead from
their perfectly straight and sure-aiming guns.*
These shooting volleys were answered by Ratcliffe's
warriors, and their reports and echoes and resound-

---

* I believe it is to this battle that Mangan refers in his
poem of " The Dark Rosaleen," when he puts the following
words into Red Hugh's mouth :—
>   " And gun peal and slogan-cry
>   Wake many a glen serene
>   Ere you shall fade, ere you shall die,
>   My dark Rosaleen.

ing thunders were heard in woods and in waters, and in the castles and stone buildings of all surrounding territories. Marvellous that the weak-hearted, yea, and the brave, too, did not flee from the conflict, hearing such battle-clangour, and the thunderings and echoings of that powerful firing, for on both sides champions were pierced and heroes slain."

Mark here, as elsewhere, the beautiful imparti-ality of our noble Four Masters. Few, if any, historians ever rivalled them in generosity and magnanimity, such their heroic love of heroism, of manly or womanly virtue, no matter what its origin or the cause in which it was exhibited. The Pro-testant and the Catholic, the Englishman and the Irishman, the Milesian chief, and Norman-Irish noble, or English courtier fresh from the Queen's smiles—all in strict proportion to their worth or unworth—are stigmatized or praised in their pure and ardent pages. Modern historians of that temper we need, and I hope yet will have as magnanimous, as just, and as veracious as that famous mediæval Four.

The Royalist vanguard, now well deployed, soon settled down steadily to their warlike work—steadily, though the nature of the ground was any-thing but favourable to straight shooting, and many a brave soldier, as he levelled his piece, found it hard even to keep his feet in the yielding soil. Under the eyes of the President and the whole army, Ratcliffe's men deployed, took rank, and fired; loaded, advanced, and fired again, ever advancing and ever firing, and the Tir-Connallians, spite their showers of arrows and spears, and the " thick volleys of red-flaming flashes " with which they responded, began to fall back, their steady ranks wavering, trembling, as it were, towards breakage and dispersion. The men had not expected that they would be required to fight to the last with Clifford's whole army now fast emerging from the wood, and getting into position behind their vanguard. They believed, and no doubt rightly believed, that their commander's instructions had been to fight and fall back, and expected momentarily to hear the bugles sing retreat. But MacDermot perceived that his handful might even so, by determined valour, defeat and destroy all Clifford's army. Could he but beat Ratcliffe and the vanguard, and drive them back in confusion upon the convoy, and then double up the convoy and the vanguard together upon the battle, what might not happen in such obstructed ground to an army left bare of its horse and encumbered with its own weight? At all events he saw his opportunity, and would not have the bugles sing retreat at all, but advance if anything, and the warpipes shriek only battle and onfall. Nothing loath, the pipers stepped out and piped.

They were brave men these pipers. The modern military band retires as its regiment goes into action. But the piper went on before his men and piped them into the thick of battle. He advanced, sounding his battle-pibroch, and stood in the ranks of war while men fell round him. Derrick in his " Image of Ireland," about this date, gives a wood-cut representing a battle. In the fore-front of the Irish lies a slain figure reflecting little credit on the artist, but under which Derrick writes " pyper," well aware that the fall of the musician was an event of importance second only to that of a considerable officer. So in the State papers we often read such entries as this : " Slew Hugh, son of Hugh, twenty-five of his men, and two pipers." " Slew Art O'Connor and his piper." A brother of Black Thomas Butler of Ormond gives a long list name by name of the rebels whom he slew. Divers pipers are specially mentioned, and in such a manner as to indicate that the slayer was particularly proud of such achievements.

So here upon the brown bog Red Hugh's pipers stood out beyond their men sounding wild and high the battle-pibrochs of the north with hearts and hands brave as any in the wild work, and the bugles sang only battle, rang battle, onfall and victory in men's hearts and ears, and the awful music of the oaths out-sang all other sounds, out-pealed the bugle-calls and battle pibrochs, the thundering of the captains rose above the thundering of the guns. Up and down, to and fro ran these, adjuring and menacing, striking and beating back the runaways. Hither and thither with swords drawn ran the Irish officers, MacDermot, lord of the Curlews, and Red Hugh's foster-brother, McSweeny of the Battle-Axes, and the two O'Gallaghers, Eocha and Tully. To and fro, up and down the wavering ranks they rushed thundering abuse, protestations, and many a fierce Irish oath and curse ; raising high the sacred name of Mary. Mary, not O'Donnell a-boo seems to have been the war-cry that day. Behind the wavering gunmen stood the lowering mailed figure of the young Oxonian, Brian Ogue and his century and a half of ranked gallowglasses, their long weapons levelled, not likely to show cowards any mercy. Silent and steady they stood to rear of all the battle clangour and confusion, a mass, though a small one, of valour educated and trained to the point of perfection ; clad in complete steel, ready to go on or go back at a word from their young chieftain, not at all ready to loose rank in either movement—flower of the Brennymen, "very great scorners of death." And again rear-ward upon some eminence stood famous Red Hugh, if we could only contrive to see him, with his blue flashing eyes and notorious fiery locks escaped from the helmet and falling on his mailed shoulders, his countenance which " no one could see without

loving," not now soft, bright and amiable as the
Four Masters beheld it when they were boys, but
stern and minatory. Somewhere far off stood Red
Hugh with his brothers, brave Rory, afterwards
Earl, one of the two who made the Flight of the
Earls and closed a great chapter of Irish history;
and Manus the well-beloved, who was to die at
home in Tir-Connall, slain by the hand of his own
rough cousin Nial Garf; and Cath-barr, "Top of
Battle," youngest of the famous four.

Then near at hand, just in the rear of the fighting
men, rode O'Rourke's bard, and MacDermot's,
and Red Hugh's as close as they might to the field
of battle, noting who were the brave and who the
recreant. The public entertain a very false notion
of the mediæval bard. They picture him as an old
bent man, with flowing white beard, sad, bowed
down in spirit, but flashing up under the influence
of liquor and the spell of poetic rage, a humble
wight receiving gifts which were a sort of alms.
Such is our modern romantic conception of the
bard. The real bard was a high-spirited, proud,
and even wealthy man, chief of a sept, and lord of
extensive estates, holding the same by right and
not by grace. If he received gifts and favours he
gave them, and his well-replenished house was open
to all comers. He was a gentleman, and ranked
with the best. When he went abroad he was as
well mounted and attended as other chiefs. He

had men of war to wait on him, though he himself
wore no arms, and never fought, for fighting was
not his function but the causing of others to fight
well. He carried no harp, and no orphan boy carried
one for him; and though he made poems and knew
poems by the hundred, he was no reciter. He went
to the wars as an observer and watcher, and men
feared him. Somewhere, I say, in the neighbour-
hood of the battle such bards, mounted on fleet
steeds, watched the progress of the fray, noting
who were the heroes and who the poltroons. And
still in the brown bog the captains thundered and
the bugles rang battle, and the banners waved
defiance and advance, and the war-pipes sounded
their shrillest and maddest, the brave pipers standing
out well in advance of the fighters. Again, through
the hearts of the wavering Tir Connallians the
fading battle-fire blazed out anew; again, with
firm mien and unbroken ranks they stood steady to
their war-work and hurled their rain of spears and
arrows, and levelled and fired their "perfectly
straight and sure-aiming guns" upon the advancing Royalists.

CHAPTER XII.

MACDERMOT BREAKS THE BATTLE ON THE QUEEN'S HOST.

ONCE again Red Hugh's men stood steady and unwavering under the Royalist fire, returning the same and with interest. The Royalists had had a long and wet march, and were not in such good condition as Red Hugh's fresh and well breakfasted troops. Now in their turn they too began to slack fire, to waver in their ranks, and finally to retreat upon the pike men, probably throwing them too into disorder. The Tir-Connaillans pressing forward began to rain their bullets into the dense ranks of the Queen's gallowglasses of the first division, who had neither cavalry nor musketeers to sweep back their assailants. So the latter at their ease poured volley after volley upon the unresisting mass.

Ratcliffe seeing that his gunmen were now beaten past the rally sought to organise a charge of his gallowglasses, crying loudly that he would head the charge himself, calling all true men to follow, and even summoning individuals by name out of the wavering and confused ranks. Meantime the

" plumbei pilluli "* of Red Hugh's " fulminators"
were pouring into the struggling crowd out of which
Ratcliffe sought to disengage the braver elements
and fashion a forlorn. Having in some sort com-
passed his purpose, though already suffering from
a shot in the face, he was leading them on " with
unconquerable resolution " when his leg was broken
by a gun-shot which brought him to a sudden halt.
So while the blood of his first wound ran down his
face, stood Ratcliffe supported in the arms of two
of his officers, † and in this situation roared to Henry
Cosby, ‡ who seems to have been next in command,
directing him to lead the charge ; but perceiving him
slack and as he was being withdrawn out of fire
he called anew to his lieutenant : " I see, Cosby,
that I must leave thee to thy baseness, but will tell
thee ere I go that it were better for thee to die by
the hands of thy countrymen than at my return to
perish by my sword." But Cosby went not on.
He was son of Francis Cosby of Stradbally Hall in
O'More's country, Cosby of the decorated tree,
and brother of Alexander who (as it was surmised)
so cleverly dodged the wild cutting and slashing of

* Philip O'Sullivan, author of these expressions, usually
mentions bullets as *glandes*. He writes of iron bullets sometimes. Musketeers he latinizes as *bombardarii,* muskets as
bombardæ. Pistols are *bombardulæ*. *Fulminatores,* he uses,
I think, for shooters of all kinds.

† One of them, Godred Tyrwhit, brother of Robert Tyrwhit
of Ketleby in Lincolnshire.

‡ He had command of a third part of the vanguard.

Rory Ogue by using his comrade as a shield. Cosby
came not on but the Tir-Connallians did. They drew
close, archers, cross-bowmen, spear-casters and
gunmen, ranked before this jammed mob of soldiers,
and slaughtered at their leisure, while flaming
Ratcliffe was being carried to the rear, and cowardly
Cosby '' showed slackness '' in leading the forlorn
which his brave commander had disengaged and
fashioned out of the clubbed vanguard.

CHAPTER XIII.

THE BRENNY MEN LET LOOSE.

THIS was the moment for a cavalry charge which
under such conditions would have cut the vanguard
to ribbons. But cavalry there were none on either
side. Neither Clifford nor Red Hugh would trust
their precious cavalry in those bogs and obstruc-
tions. But in the rear of MacDermot's men there
was something as good, better in such ground as
this.   Here in shining ranks stood O'Rourke's
Brenny men standing at their ease watching the
fray, waiting for one word from their chief. At last
the word came, literally a word. Brian Ogue, in
tones not familiar to the class-rooms of Oxford,
where not long since Brian Ogue of the Battle-
Axes O'Rourke did nonsense verses or boggled

over the mysteries of *Barbara, Celarent, Darii
Ferioque priores* and the irregular verbs of Lily's
Latin grammar,* shouted Farragh. " Farragh ! "
he cried now, not Ferio, and like hounds slipped
from the leash, O'Rourke's Brenny men went upon
the Queen's vanguard. Only 160, but mailed
gallowglasses, picked men and strong, the flower
of Breffney, all in rank perfectly fresh, eager as
hounds certain of victory. MacDermot's gunmen
and archers gave way to the right hand and the
left, opening out like folding-doors as the Brennymen with a shout which at such an instant changed
fortitude to alarm and alarm to panic terror, went
upon the foe.

The battle harvest was ripe and these were the
reapers ; ripened, if I may say so, by that rain of
darts and spears and heat of " red-flaming flashes "
and fiery balls of lead. Guess how coward Cosby,
who showed slackness in charging the gunmen, met
this forward-sweeping wave of steel, with its crest
of glittering axes. Cosby and his forlorn quickly fell
back as if there were any hope in demoralized
numbers, terrified yet more by the retreat of the
only corps which still showed some rudiments of
formation. The vanguard was hopelessly clubbed,
gunmen and halberdiers inextricably entangled.

* " It was ordered that no Latin grammar but Lily's should
be taught in this kingdom, in order to assimilate the in-
struction of youth in the two countries, A.D. 1587."—*Sir
James Ware's Annals.*

Nor at this juncture had they a leader to disentwine the tangle and pull the lines straight and distinct. The vanguard was captainless, reduced to that disastrous state by Ratcliffe's broken leg and Cosby's lily heart. Brave men, surely abundant enough even now in this wild moment, had no chance, mobbed, overborne by the cowards, unable to find each other out in the press and stand together disengaged from the ruck. What chance ever have the brave left captainless—what fate but be trampled down by the fools and cowards? Had that random bullet but spared their captain's shank-bone things might have been so different. Were he at this moment to return as he had promised, and, as he had promised, run his blade through Cosby for a swift and salutary beginning, he, standing clear of the chaos, would have gathered all these to himself, crying to them in general and calling men by their names. But the Mac-an-Iarla was well on his way to the rear now. Brave Ratcliffe was gone and Cosby's lily heart struck work while his shaking knees were already turning to flight and the vanguard was hopelessly clubbed and the yelled " Farragh " of the Brennymen clove all ears and hearts.

To left and right MacDermot and his gunmen opened out like double doors unfolding as Brian Ogue went into the Queen's vanguard. To left and right they opened and now poured in their fire transversly on either flank of the struggling mass, while in front Brian Ogue and his reapers fell to the despatch of their red work. A moment the raised axes, razor-sharp and bright, glistened in the sun, then fell ringing with dry clangour or more horribly silent, rising not so bright, rising and falling like lightning, such a war harvest to be reaped, such battle-fury in men's hearts, and such an opportunity !

And on the flanks MacDermot volleyed transversely, and soon his spear-hurlers clutched sword and fell on, and the gunmen slung the slow calyver, gripped sword-hilt and did likewise.

Not long the struggle under such conditions. Back rolled the vanguard, back on the battle where Clifford was ranking his men and making his dispositions, seeing how matters went in front. Back rolled the vanguard, effusing afar their own panic, back in the first instance on the forward convoy. Here the peasants cut their wagon traces, mounted and ran, and the trains of mules and pack horses stampeded, and amid this confusion the flying vanguard tumbled into through and over the battle, while brave Clifford did all that man could do to stem the raging flood, and MacDermot's prophetic soul was justified by the event. He had doubled back the vanguard and the first convoy upon the battle. And the battle too was broken and rolled back on the second convoy and the rearguard.

CHAPTER XIV.

CLIFFORD'S HEROIC DEATH.

At this moment a cry arose : " The President is dead !" The President had gone down in the midst of the raging flood, but he was not killed. His horse was shot, and he had fallen. He was soon on his feet again roaring commands and encouragements to his own men so far as they were still rational beings, endeavouring in vain to restore the fight, commanding, entreating, doing all that a brave man could do. " There had not come of the English into Ireland in the latter days a better man."

Seeing the day utterly lost, two of his Irish officers, the lieutenant of Captain Burke, name not given, and Sir Miler McSweeny urged him to leave the field. " Overcome with wrath and shame, he declared, Roman-like, that he would not overlive that day's ignominy. But that affection which moved Sir Miler McSweeny to use entreatyes persuaded him now to practiz force, by which they caryed him from the pursewing rebells some few paces, when enraged with the vildness of his men, which he often repeated, he brake from them in a fury, and turning head alone, made head to the whole troopes of pursewers, in the midst of whom when he was stroake through the bodye with a bullet* he died fighting, consecrating by an admyrable resolucion the memory of his name to immortality and leaving the example of his vertue to be intytuled by all honourable posterities."†

Yet, even after Clifford's death his division or parts of it rallied and fought on. Savage and the rearguard managed to keep their ranks while the roaring deluge of flight and panic terror raged past them. There was tough fighting, or at all events resistance of some sort, after the fall of Clifford, and before the best materials of the Queen's host gave way utterly, and the rout became universal. Savage, I feel sure, played a brave part ; I should be much surprised if he did not, for gallantry was in his blood. Four centuries had elapsed since the founder of the clan Savage marched from Dublin with the great John de Courcy and a handful of Norman knights and archers to the conquest of Ulster, and did conquer Ulster. And de Courcy

---

* Dymok says by a pike. He was slain by a bullet; the pike-thrust was given afterwards as the victors ran past. The account given by the Four Masters is doubtless correct. Sir Miler lived afterwards in Tir-Connall, where he must have related to many the exact manner of Clifford's death. In Tir-Connall the Annals were written, and quite possibly the Four Masters knew Sir Miler and talked with him.

† Philip O'Sullivan says that he offered these gentlemen great rewards if they would see him safe out of the battle, and that he fled a considerable distance. This is absurd. Dymok's account is more in keeping with all that we know about this brave and chivalrous gentleman.

planted the Savage in the north of Dal-Aradia* as
one of his barons, and there for four centuries, while
houses rose and fell, many a wild storm of war,
Edward Bruce's invasion amongst them, broke upon
but broke not this hardy Norman-Irish clan. They
were Queen's men now, and Sir Arthur was their
most distinguished representative. He served the
Crown in honourable posts after this rout in the
Curlews, and behaved with gallantry and distinction in the Battle of Kinsale in 1602.† Savage,
surely, like Clifford and Ratcliffe, did his best to
save the battle, but at last all broke and fled, Brian
Ogue's battle-axes going like smiths' hammers or
the flails of threshing-men on their rear and Mac
Dermot volleying from right to left, and all solid
companies getting broken up and swept away by
the torrents of panic-stricken humanity. So at last
the whole of the Queen's host was reduced to
chaos, streaming madly away, and the Battle of
the Curlew Mountains was fought and lost and won.
On rushed the fugitives, disappearing not too
rapidly within that half mile of autumnal forest.
The road was choked with baggage-waggons,
provisions, camp-furniture, impedimenta of various
kinds, and the running masses of men collided and
jostled against each other and the trees, as the

* Co. Down.

† *Pacata Hibernia,* last chapters, where his name is several
times mentioned with honour.

Royalists re-travelled these primeval solitudes, while battle-axe and sword and calyver and pistol played ever on their rear.

CHAPTER XV.

MARKHAM STRIKES IN WITH THE QUEEN'S HORSEMEN.

As the runaways emerged from the southern fringes of the forest a sight was presented fit to recall to a sense of shame and obedience to their captains the minds of men not utterly frenzied and unmanned by fear. Before them if they could see anything for fright lay the great brown bog threaded by its narrow white road gorse-fringed, and on the road the clear midday sunlight glancing from bright morions and armour, the Earl of Southampton's horse advancing under the command of Sir Griffin Markham ; quietly, leisurely following Sir Conyers under full belief that the passage of the Curlews had been forced, riding four or five abreast along the road which wound through the great bog that intervened between the wood and '' the barricado with doble flanckes.'' What a spectacle for their brave commander when the wood suddenly began to spout its rills and torrents of wild runaways, kerne, gallowglasse, musketeers, common soldiers, and officers tumbling out thence in every direction, falling into peat-holes, and rising and running, the better part without weapons, many tearing off and flinging away their armour as they ran.

Markham, a brave men who had a head for war and also an eye in his head, at a glance took in the situation and decided swiftly on his course. When he first witnessed the extraordinary spectacle far out in front at the other side of the great bog—viz., the green wood vomiting forth at a hundred points the whole Royalist army which was to have conquered North Connaught, he was not far from that "barricado with doble flanckes," and advancing along the main road which swerved so much, stretching across the bog like a bent bow. But besides this wheel-way there was, as formerly mentioned, another way more direct.

It was a mere continuity of moderately firm ground, rocky and furze-strewn, solid enough for his purpose, which fell in with the main road on this side of the wood. Quickly taking in the situation, he advanced as well as he could, and as swiftly, along this rough short-cut by which the panic-stricken army did not run, and which was open to his use. The poor wretches, for the most part, poured along and on both sides of the main road. So avoiding that shameful torrent of wild humanity, he and his dragoons by this short cut struck in upon

the main road behind them, between the runaways
and the pursuers. Here Markham formed his men
on the road and on both sides of it, the ground being
firm enough and charged MacDermot and his gunmen, now disordered in pursuit ; charged them, and
also broke them, cutting them down in all directions
or driving them into the wood and far out into the
wetnesses of the bog. Now was the time for Captain
Burke, Sir Miler McSweeny or some other brave
and competent officer to take charge of that roaring
flood of ruin, and re-order such of its elements as
were not utterly demoralised ; for the pursuit was
stayed, and the pursuers in their turn overthrown
by brave Markham and the cavalry.

CHAPTER XVI.

IS COUNTER-CHARGED BY THE OXONIAN.

MARKHAM'S spirited charge gave an opportunity
of converting the rout into a victory. MacDermot
and his gunmen were now shattered and dispersed,
driven out into the bog on both sides of that firm
ground where Markham had charged. But now
while the Royalist dragoons rushed along, sabring
and spearing, their ranks quite disordered in pursuit,
and while some stood firing pistol shots at the

gunmen out in the bog, Markham and his horse
came full tilt upon a new and unexpected foe. From
the wood emerged Brian Ogue with his century
and a half of heavy-armed foot, steady, ranked, in
perfect order. Fearing the event, Brian Ogue kept
his gallowglasse well in hand, and here, following
with slow deliberate foot in the rear of the kerne,
emerged to sight. From the green forest came to
sudden view that formidable phalanx, their shining
battle-axes now dull enough. The Royalist horse
were now charged in front by Brian Ogue, while
MacDermot's gunmen closing in from the bogs
fired transversely through their ranks from each
side. Markham and the horse could not win the
batt: ₃ alone. Then as now, horse were no match
for foot that would keep their ranks and decline to
be frightened by mere show and glitter. Charged
by Brian Ogue, Markham could not stand the impact of the Brenny men. Down tumbled horses and
their riders to the cleaving of Brian Ogue's battle-
axes. Markham too was utterly routed, so routed
that he lost " all his pennons and guidons." Brian
Ogue handled the Queen's horsemen that day
better than I think he ever handled Lily's irregular
Latin verbs at Oxford.

There was another Oxford man, but of the
Queen's Irish in this battle, Richard Burke, Lord
Dunkellin, chief designate of the High Burkes.
Brian Ogue in this melee received two wounds, one

in the hand and another in the leg. Markham did not escape without receiving some tokens. He had the small bone of his right arm broken " with the stroake of a bullet " and his clothes torn by another.

So the cavalry too broke and fled, following the fugitives, and again the flood of flight and chase rolled down the slopes of the Curlews. The guard so prudently planted at the barricado participated in the disgraceful rout, which was perhaps the most remarkable example of cowardice in this whole shameful business.

They were 160 in number and might have held the pass for hours against any army unprovided with artillery. Clifford had not destroyed the barricado, but merely opened a passage through it. The gap was narrow enough for defence and not wide enough for the torrent of ruin which now sought to pour through. Some wiser than the rest clambered over the rampart and the bristling palisades. Most of the fugitives rushed at the open passage and blocked it. But for the relief afforded by Markham there would have been an awful slaughter here.

Of the beaten army the Meath Irish fared worst. The great mass of the army were Connaught Irish, who were well acquainted with the Curlews and knew good paths over the bogs and through the hills. Many of their officers and lords had, I

suppose, been often here hawking. The Meath
Irish knew nothing of the country, and so thought
of nothing save of rushing straight along by the
way they came. The few English soldiers here
shared their fate. They were certainly few. As we
have seen, Bingham had purged the Connaught
army of Englishmen. Bingham meant no slight
upon English valour which was and is as good as
any in the world, but when English recruits were
scarecrows, with whom Falstaff " would not march
through Coventry," " a great many diseased, and
many mad,"* what other course was possible for
Bingham contending for his life and honour against
Red Hugh, and Granuaile's son, and MacDermot
of the Curlews, and Brian Ogue and divers other
fire-breathing dragons of the West?

These timber barriers which the Royalists had
passed so joyfully that morning proved now an
obstacle to their flight. Here, those who still kept
their weapons flung them away, and here also
quantities of clothes and armour were found. The
pursuers consisted only of the 600 fulminators, now
reduced to less than 400, and Brian Ogue's century
and a half of gallowglasses. But resistance was
never thought of.

From the mountains the mingled flood of chase

* These are the words of the Mayor of Chester, who received and forwarded to Ireland those astonishing levies.
Even in great Eliza's golden time, there was an incredible
amount of folly at headquarters.

and panic-flight rolled towards the town of Boyle, execution never ceasing, for Sir Griffin seems not to have been able again to get his cavalry into order. Through the gates of Boyle it poured, and kept pouring, till the gates had to be closed against the foe. Red Hugh's lieutenants and their warriors encamped that night under or not far from the walls, and one of the most remarkable battles recorded in Irish history came to an end. In war there is a great deal of luck, and we may observe, too, that scratch armies are admirably fitted for the losing of battles. Here were Meathian Irish and Connaught Irish—men one might almost describe, such was the disjointed state of the land, as of different nationalities ; here veterans of the army of Essex, and soldiers drawn from the garrisons ; here, finally, were English soldiers mixed with Irish, and the Irish for the most part not regulars, only the rising-out of Meath and Connaught, that is to say, the local gentry and their followers. Yet the little band of conquerors was a scratch army too, so from any point of view it must be accounted a most glorious victory.

The battle was won by 600 musketeers and archers, and a company of Breffneian gallowglasse. A very remarkable battle in every way ; lost to the Crown seemingly through the cowardice of the Royalist vanguard, or shall we say, of Henry Cosby, who, we may hope, got well killed. In this battle there were slain of the Royalists one thousand four hundred, no quarter being given. MacDermot and Brian Ogue lost in killed and wounded only 240 men. The baggage, standards, etc., and nearly all the arms of the invading army, fell into the hands of the conquerors.

When in reading English history we perceive the intense wrath felt in London against the Earl of Essex and his conduct of the Irish wars, we must remember the sense of imperial humiliation which was felt at a defeat such as the foregoing sustained under his government. The Nine Years' War is throughout a wonder, miraculous everywhere. From beginning to end the insurgent lords only lost one battle, the battle of Kinsale. Yet they were beaten !

CHAPTER XVII.

A CUSTOM OF THE AGE.

BRIAN OGUE, as stated, received two bullet wounds during his victorious tussle with Markham and the horse. He rode or was borne in a litter homewards to the camp along that corpse-strewn road. His scratches don't seem to have troubled him much. He paused as he went, scrutinizing with deliberation the bodies of those who by their superior armour seemed men of rank, and which were exhibited to him as he passed. Amongst them he was shown the familiar features of Sir Conyers Clifford, President of Connaught. He knew him well. He had been to visit him on his first coming into his Presidentia, and had only been prevented from allying himself and his Breffneian nation with the Queen's cause by the stern menacing attitude assumed towards him by Red Hugh. He ordered his attendants to behead Clifford, and sent the head forward as a trophy and token to Red Hugh. The decapitation of slain foes was a universal custom of the age. Had Brian Ogue fallen, Clifford would have decapitated him. Among the rows of heads which adorned the battlements of Dublin Castle at this moment was the tarred head of Brian Ogue's own father, the brave proud Brian na Murtha. Clifford's head was forwarded to Red Hugh in the north; his body was conveyed south to Mac Dermot, to the Castle of Gaywash, hard by Boyle, where MacDermot and his army were now encamped.

I like Brian Ogue and am sorry, custom or no custom, that he ordered the decapitation of Clifford. My regret has been anticipated by the Four Masters.

Red Hugh sent a swift detachment of horse with Clifford's head to Collooney, to Nial Garf, his cousin in command there. Nial Garf, demanding a

parley with the defenders of the Castle, informed
Sir Donough of the defeat of the Royalists, and in
proof of the statement exhibited the head of the
slain general. That was enough. Sir Donough
gave up Collooney, and himself and its defenders as
prisoners without demanding terms, for his
condition was desperate. Shortly after Red Hugh
himself appeared upon the scene, and held a long
colloquy with his captive. The result of this conference was that Sir Donough undertook to transfer
his allegiance from the Queen to Red Hugh, and
to hold all Sligo from him on the same terms that
his ancestors used to hold it* from Red Hugh's
ancestors. Hugh reinvested him in the lordship of
Sligo, presented him with horses, cattle, sheep,
ploughs, and all manner of farm instruments, and
even with a population, so that in a short time the
wasted land became once again an inhabited, in-
dustrious and well-settled principality. Red Hugh
gave him what the Crown first would not, and then
could not give him—viz., the estates of his
ancestors. Hugh took his hostages and thence-
forward directed all his motions. I may add that
subsequently, when troubles began to close round
the young chief of Tir-Connall, Sir Donough took
to intriguing anew with the Queen's party, and

* One was that three bards, all nominated in the deed,
should satirize the party who first broke contract. Modern
times were coming but had not yet come.

Red Hugh had to imprison Sir Donough, and raise his brother to the chieftaincy.

Granuaile's son, Burke the Marine, long rocking idly before the ruins of Sligo Castle, weighed anchor and sailed with all his lime, cannons and provisions. I dare say he annexed them, for I find that he now transferred his allegiance to the victorious Red Hugh. The land Burke having watched grimly the sinking sails of his cousin, marched back to his principality of Mayo, ruling and regulating there as Red Hugh's MacWilliam.

Released from his formidable opponent, Clifford, Red Hugh resumed his operations speedily, made himself virtual master of Connaught, and meditated now the overthrow of Thomond and the O'Briens.

CHAPTER XIX.

MACDERMOT'S LATIN LETTER.

As mentioned, the headless body of the President was carried southwards to MacDermot. The treatment which it received at his hands will be perceived from the following curious letter, despatched probably a day or two after the battle, by that chieftain, to the Constable of Boyle. It fell into the hands of Sir John Harrington, and was

published by him in his *Nugae Antiquae*. It is by
him " censured " justly enough, to be " barbarous
for the Latyn, but cyvill for the sence " :

" *Conestabulario de Boyle salutem.*

*Scias quod ego traduxi corpus gubernatoris ad
monasteriu Sanctae Trinitatis propter ejus dilec-
tionem, et alia de causa. Si velitis mihi redire meos
captivos ex praedicto corpore quod paratus sum
ad conferendum vobis ipsum; alias sepultus erit
honeste in predicto monasterio et sic vale, scriptu
apud Gaywash,* 15 *August,* 1599 ; *interim pone
bonu linteamentum ad prædictum corpus, et si
velitis sepelire omnes alios nobiles non impediam
vos erga eos.*

" *Mac Dermon.*"

Probable translation of the foregoing :

" To the Constable of Boyle, greeting.

" Know that I have surrendered the body of the
Governor to the Monastery of the Holy Trinity, on
account of his command and for other cause. If
you wish to restore me my captives in return for the
aforesaid body, I am ready to confer with you in
person. In any case, he will be honourably interred
in the aforesaid monastery. So fare thee well.

" Written at Gaywash, August 15, 1599.

" In the meantime wrap [I have wrapped] a
good shroud round the aforesaid body, and if you

wish to bury all the other nobles, I will not interfere with your doing so.''

Note the aristocratic feeling expressed here : MacDermot seems to think that the Constable would only be at the pains of burying the bodies of the gentlemen. The " *redire meos captivos* " is funny enough, but the letter is the letter of a soldier and a gentleman.

Dymok adds the following, which has some interest, though inconsiderable.

'' By this lettre is too truly interpreted a troublesome dream of the Governor's, which he had about a yeare before this defeat, when being awakened by his wife out of an unquiet sleepe, he recounted unto her that he thought himself to have been taken prisoner by O'Donnell, and that certen religious men of compassion conveied him into their monastery, where they concealed him. And so indeed, as he dreamed, or rather prophesied, the monastery hath his bodye, the worlde his fame, and his friends the want of his virtu.''

GLOSSARY

Barbara, Celarent Darii Ferioque priores, Mnemonic verses to help in learning logic.

CAPPED, saluted.

COIGNE AND LIVERY, forcible billeting of troops.

CRANNOG, lake dwelling.

De facto, in fact.

De jure, in law, or by law.

FARRAGH! an Irish war cry.

GALLOWGLASSE, heavy-armed Irish soldiers.

GARRANS, work horses, hacks.

GRIFE, dyke or ditch.

In tail male, to male heirs only.

KERNE, light-armed Irish soldiers.

Kudos, glory, fame.

LANG SYNE, long since, long ago.

LEECHES, doctors.

MEARINGS, borders.

MELEE, a fight or scuffle.

METHER, a vessel for drinking out of.

PIBROCHS, war pipe tunes.

Redire meos captivos, Restore me my captives.

SAGA, a tale, a history—(Norse).

TANISTRY. The law or custom of appointing a successor during the life of the present holder of the chiefship or lands.